CW01402136

103724411

GAMES OF CHANCE

BY THE SAME AUTHOR

Morning
A Letter
Memoir in the Middle of the Journey
Gabriel Young
Tug-of-War
Hounds of Spring
Happy Endings
Revolution Island
Gentleman's Gentleman
Memories of My Mother
Rules of Life
Cautionary Tales for Women
Hope Cottage
Best Friends
Small Change
Eleanor
The Duchess of Castile
His Christmas Box
Money Matters
The Social Comedy
Evening
Tales of Love and War
Byron's Diary
The Stepmother
The Sodbury Crucifix
Damnation

The Collected Works of Julian Fane
Volumes I, II, III, IV & V

The Harlequin Edition

Three Stories of Boyhood
Secrets of the Confessional
A Reader's Choice
A Writer's Life for Me
How to Publish Yourself
A Bad Experience
Mistress of Arts
Can Women Say No?
Ralph's Religion
How to be a Writer
Snobs
The Harrison Archive
In Short

GAMES OF CHANCE

The History of a Family

Julian Fane

The Book Guild Ltd
Sussex, England

First published in Great Britain in 2005 by
The Book Guild Ltd
25 High Street
Lewes, East Sussex
BN7 2LU

Typesetting in Garamond by
Keyboard Services, Luton, Bedfordshire

Printed in Great Britain by
Antony Rowe Ltd, Chippenham, Wiltshire

A catalogue record for this book is available from
The British Library

ISBN 1 85776 874 4

To
Robert Sheaf and Val May
my honorary cousins

Contents

What Stirred in the Forest   1

The First Rung   21

The Touch of Royalty   43

Topsy-Turvy   69

Both Sides of the Medal   97

The Apogee   119

Two and Three   143

An Idiot   169

Blessings in Disguise   201

Square One   233

What Stirred in The Forest

Long ago, in one of the hiding places of history, a hamlet existed. It had no church, and was more like a settlement or an encampment than a hamlet. It was located in a forest with an unoriginal name, the Forest of Woody, and outsiders called it Wood Houses; but very few people from outside had reason to refer to it, let alone visit, and for the inhabitants it was simply home.

Such inhabitants amounted to round about fifty as a rule. If winter was long and hard, more babies were born in summer and the population increased. But the extra mouths to feed meant that some of the older generation died sooner than they might have done. Thus nature controlled the number of members of the human species it could support.

The living in Wood Houses was primitive, even savage, compared with the circumstances prevailing in the countryside of England. Its location, more accurately, was a clearing in several thousand acres of woodland: there was a spring of water and not much else, and only rudimentary drainage. The 'houses' resembled sheds rudely thatched with straw – the shelters put up by foresters had been enlarged and shaped into dwellings for families. Even farther back in time, the woodworkers had won the right to cut down enough trees to provide space for habitable accommodation and vegetable patches.

That right was won from a Squire Dunbee of Gorham. The Dunbees were a farming dynasty, and had branched out into timber. One Dunbee bought a bit of the Forest of Woody, another discovered that professional itinerant foresters did not come cheap, and a third, the present Squire, devised a system of profit-sharing from which all benefited. The people of Wood Houses lived rent free, were allowed to poach game in moderation, and could sell the Dunbees' wood in various shapes and forms, then had to give the Squire half the money they earned in each quarter of the year. They were allowed a free hand in theory, and were not bothered unduly by their master, but in practice their husbandry of his trees was supervised, he also kept accounts, he had eyes in the back of his head, and men ready to beat and even to hang anybody who tried to cheat him.

The laws of the land supported the strong and were down on the weak in Merrie England. Life was dangerous, life was cheap, but in the wider world beyond the trees robber bands operated, press-gangs stole men away, knights and lords played war games, and non-stop epidemics gave the Grisly Reaper extra excuses to swing his scythe. Wood Houses was a refuge as well as a job. The Squire and his minions were a quarterly threat; but he sent a cart to carry wood to whoever ordered it, he stuck to his side of the bargain, and donated a cask of ale at Christmas. Existence within a forest was dull; but it was safer than elsewhere. The men were satisfied by acquiring and exercising their skill with axes and saws, at felling and planting, and the women and children helped with picking up wood-chips, cutting hazel twigs for pea-sticks, tending the livestock and finding the food of the forest, fungi, nuts, berries, green shoots. And they had their excitements, a rare day out to Gorham or Bushton, the killing of the community pig.

Necessity proved itself the mother of invention at Wood Houses. A reliable leader was required to enforce discipline and maintain the status quo: several heads of the Stone family filled the bill. Silas Stone, a middle-aged greybeard, strong in body and mind, now followed in the footsteps of his father and grandfather. He organised the schedules of work, and dealt with monetary business. He was respected by Squire Dunbee, and was appreciated by his fellow-residents. His wife Jane ran the schooling of children, their son Jonathan was in charge of recreational fixtures, for instance the May Day revels. The Stones also ministered to the sick, and Silas led the walk to and from church in Gorham on Sundays, and buried the dead.

Gradually 'modern' conveniences were introduced to Wood Houses. Front doors on leather hinges opened and shut, replacing doors of boards that had to be lifted in and out of the embrasure. Brick chimneys sucked the smoke out of living rooms. Strong garden fences were built to keep the deer at bay, and more vegetables could then be grown. Fencing safeguarded edible domestic creatures, poultry in particular.

The attractions of Wood Houses were not merely negative. Because existence there was a battle, not many inhabitants lived to be middle-aged, let alone old by current standards: it was therefore reserved for youth. Optimism and high spirits were the order of every day – Silas Stone had his advanced age of fifty on the side of his authority. The very air seemed to be romantic, for the boys and girls had to provide entertainment for one another. Marriages were happy for a similar reason, husbands and wives would have died of boredom, especially in winter, if they were not enjoying themselves in their basic versions of beds.

The Forest of Woody was beautiful into the bargain – at least when rain did not drip down from leaden skies. The boles of the great trees towered pillar-like and patiently around the homes of the midgets who would one day cut them to the ground. Some were grey and smooth, some rough of bark, some split, affording lodging for bats and bees; and saplings sprouted in their shade. They provided a green canopy in summer, and in winter a carpet of russet leaves. In all seasons, the sun shone between them, in mote-filled rays of dappling beams.

The people of the Forest were not aesthetes.

Beauty was not a word much used, except possibly to describe a fat duckling. Yet maybe they were influenced unconsciously to live in such uncomfortable conditions in the back of beyond by the pleasures available to the eye. Perhaps the music of the axes in daytime appealed to their ears.

Longevity was a word unknown and unused in Wood Houses. Invalidity was dreaded both by potential invalids and by their relations: uselessness seemed not to deserve a share of the hard-earned food of a family. Cruelty was a phenomenon barely recognised by country folk, or, for that matter, by anybody anywhere in those days. The ethics of the people of Woody were animalic – the old were advised to make themselves scarce in blunt terms. Caring children might wheel a parent in a sort of wheelbarrow and dump him or her near the Charity Hall of Gorham. The aged parents of children who did not care were apt to expire unexpectedly or fail to return from strolls into the Forest.

An exception to the rule was a widow woman surviving into the middle of a seventh decade. She was said to be too awkward to lie down and die. She had always offended against the conventions of Wood Houses. She had been a rebellious child, a nasty girl, a shrew of a wife, and barren to boot. She was a bad neighbour, had a wicked tongue, swore at children, picked quarrels and got into fights, even physical fights with other women, and always had a razor-sharp little axe hooked into the leather belt she knotted round her middle. She was called a bitch and hated. She was called a witch and feared. Her married name was Widdle.

Surnames in Wood Houses were changeable. They described the men who bore them: for instance, Dick Carter owned the wheeled vehicle that carried wood out of the forest, while James Stacker made the wood ready for collection by Squire Dunbee's labourers. The Stone family possessed a lump of rock on which axes could be ground better than in any other way. The hamlet had a Baker for obvious reasons, a Quick who swung his axe with particular rapidity, a Lightfoot who could dance, and a Waterman who kept the stream clear and the spring at its source correctly channelled. All such names were subject to alteration: thus, Dan Quick's grand-father had been called Cockerell, because he supplied chickens and eggs, and Joe Baker's late father had been Manners or Manures, again for obvious reasons.

The name Widdle referred to micturition. Jimmy Widdle earned it in childhood, his contemporaries nicknamed him on account of his weak bladder, and, although his father had been a respectable axeman called Lopper, the nickname turned into Jimmy's surname owing to his feeble physique as well as his waterworks.

How he came to marry a virago was a mystery. She chose him, of course – he was too frightened of her to do otherwise than to come to heel –

but she could have done better. Difficult though it might be to see good looks in the beaky bony weatherbeaten features of her later life, she had been attractive once upon a time. As Mildred Skinner, aged sixteen, she was slim and had a fierce face with the eyes of a predatory bird. The braver boys tackled her in a romantic sense.

'Like a walk, pretty? ... Dare you to walk in the woods with me ... Race you to the hollow tree where we wouldn't be seen ... It's mistletoe time, Mildred!'

'I'd rather be dead than walk with you,' she snapped back. 'I'll dare to kick you where it hurts. Yes, come under the mistletoe and let me wring your neck, cocky!'

The explanations of her marriage in modern terms were that she was drawn to the differences between Jimmy and herself, that they somehow complemented each other, that she was thoroughly perverse and he was her whipping boy.

Certainly, after they were married by the Rector of Gorham who happened to call at Woody one morning to order logs for his fire, she never showed sympathy for her husband. The naughty forecast was that Jimmy would not be able to consummate the marriage or supply the later demands of her wiry physique, and in due course Mildred levelled similar accusations.

She cursed him audibly and constantly. He was a 'widdling' this and a 'widdling' that, a pitiful 'widdler', and no good to man, woman or beast: the latter charge was untrue in part, for in fact he was clever at splitting a treetrunk.

Poor Jimmy Widdle, he died young not of being hen-pecked, as had been expected, but of an accident at work. He was swinging his 'dummer', the heavy wooden sledgehammer used for driving wedges into lengths of treetrunk in order to split them into portable sections. He hoisted the dummer off the ground, swung it high, the 'dum' detached itself from the handle, dropped on his skull and cracked it open. According to foresters working nearby, he lived long enough to say to them, 'That's a funny thing' – his last words.

Mildred was not amused. She jeered at him in death, too. Her form of obituary of her husband was to say to mourners at his funeral, 'He couldn't even stick two pieces of wood together.'

Her parents died soon after their son-in-law. A winter's bane carried them away – they were amongst the usual casualties of cold and dark winter months.

Mildred was alone. She earned a living by taking over the work of her father, skinning animals and curing their skins for people to cobble together into garments. Her residence was always hung about with dead rabbits, weasels, squirrels and rats, and with their pelts on wooden stretchers exposed to the elements to dry and soften. She reverted to her maiden surname, Skinner. She also profited from her knowledge of where wild strawberries grew, and bees stored their honey, and pheasants laid their eggs, and the best young nettles were available. She sold herbal remedies along with luxury foodstuffs. A black iron pot boiled in her living room and the steam smelt as poisonous as the brew was generally said to be. The suspicion that she was a witch, or at least godless, gained ground, and kept her critics at bay.

She aged without grace. At sixty she was fitter than some at forty, and more prickly and rude. Her skin looked as dry as those she had torn off animals and rubbed with special salts. One winter she coughed so hard that it disturbed the sleep of neighbours, and Silas Stone advised her to go for charity at Gorham: he got a flea in his ear.

On Sundays she seemed to show she was no longer right in the head by deriding and ridiculing her neighbours going to church.

'You'll wear your feet out for nowt,' she shrilled at them. 'You'll rot in hell just the same!'

She stooped to hurl at them the insults of the day: 'Cowpats! Pisspots!'

And although they were on their way to the House of God some of them hurled back at her the jibes that hurt her most, for example 'Mother Widdle!' because she had never borne a child, and then, 'Bloody fingers!' because of her skinning.

It happened in Maytime.

Mildred Skinner walked into the woods according to custom. She was attired as usual, in a sack-like dress reaching to her ankles made of some faded and patched blue material, a shawl of real loose-woven sacking over her shoulders and gathered by a pin of bone at her neck, another shawl round her waist, her leather belt with the bright-bladed axe hooked in it, and no shoes on her brown and calloused feet. A capacious bag of the blue material was slung across her flat chest. The thumb of her left hand fitted into the V at the top of her tall stick; her right hand was free to seize the axe if need be.

There was nothing strange in any of these circumstances.

Mildred followed the path made by the foresters and by their haulage of wood. She passed by some of them, already chopping and sawing; but no greetings were exchanged. When the path petered out she dived into a part of the forest where weeds and brambles held sway, and she felt at home.

She began to wind her way round obstacles, bending under branches, clambering over fallen trees, treading carefully for fear of snakes on dry ground and quagmires under wet cushions of green moss. She proceeded like an animal, warily, watchfully, her sharp eyes wide so that she should miss nothing. Now she paused, studied the ground, stooped to pick a shy herb, continued, reached into a hole in a hollow tree but drew a blank, and frightened a bird off its nest in a thick bush and pinched a few of its eggs, not all, for she wanted young birds to be born and to lay more eggs for her in another year.

She did not know where Squire Dunbee's woodland ended, and the property of other owners of the forest began. She neither knew nor cared: she was invisible, no one would find her, anyway the rights and wrongs of the rich were beyond her ken.

She was not impervious to the weather. The shafts of sunlight filtered by the leaves of trees gave her pleasure, and the sensual balminess was better than rain and storm or snow that concealed the eatables she sought. She wandered farther into the wood, not forgetting to keep an eye on the sun which would guide her back to Woody. She came across a tinkling streamlet, fringed with watercress. She half-filled her bag with the cress, and at noon she sat down on the low bough of a tree with her back against the bole and ate a biscuity piece of bread with some of the cress.

Drowsiness set upon her. She kept on losing the thread of her thoughts. She was rumoured to have been raped by wild men in these remoter regions of the forest, and perhaps she remembered the episode with mixed feelings. Perhaps she regretted Jimmy Widdle, his life and his death. Birds sang their challenges from the treetops, and bumblebees rumbled by. A dog barked in the distance.

The sound that woke her was different. It was not loud, but should not have been audible in uninhabited woodland. She thought it was a household cat, and that boys had lost it here on purpose. She thought it might be an animal in a trap: if so, she would kill it, carry it home, skin and eat it for supper. The sound was a mixture of whimper and gurgle.

She moved towards it cautiously – it could be the bait in a trap to catch herself. She stopped at the edge of an almost circular glade. A tall tree grew in the glade – it had out-reaching branches that bowed down earthwards because of their weight. The sound seemed to come from the direction of the tree; and now Mildred spotted a shape that was not arboreal amongst its lower branches. Something hung from a branch, a bag, a sack, an elongated sack with a bulge at the bottom swaying to and fro in the breeze and as the branch shook.

She stayed still. She was sure she would be jumped on if she approached the sack. She was too old and suspicious to fall for a trick. But she did not retreat, she was too curious to get out of harm's way. Time passed, and she heard neither lowered voices nor the crack of a twig underfoot – she heard only that peculiar noise and the backing of birdsong and the normal rustle of life in woods.

At last she jumped to a conclusion. She acted against her principles and walked over to the sack. It was tied to the branch, and her idea was that it could not have been where it was for long. How could she have failed to hear the person who tied the knot? Where was that person? Was she being watched? She drew her axe from her belt and cut the hempen cord. She lowered the sack to the ground, looked in and saw the baby.

She had eventually thought the bulge was a baby, and she hated babies. But she had taken the risk of crossing the glade and cutting down the sack. And now, under untypical compulsion, she scuffled into the undergrowth with sack and baby, and loped away from that glade as quickly as her legs would carry her.

Eventually she paused to get her breath back. She was out of danger, she hoped – nobody had followed her. But she was stuck with the baby. She probably should have left it to whimper and gurgle to death. She extracted it from the sack.

It was wrapped in a cloth, and clean – it cannot have been in the sack for long. It was brown-skinned and blue-eyed, and a boy, a boy a day or two old. He was not obviously hungry – he uttered not a sound. He opened his arms as if to embrace her. She folded the sack and put it on top of the watercress in her bag, and laid the baby boy in his cloth on the sack, and swivelled the bag over her shoulder. She headed for Woody. The boy might be worth money.

Women and children were out and about in the afternoon sunshine. When the boy began to cry, they blocked Mildred's path to her home. They did not get too close – somebody suggested she had her witch's cat in the bag. Others asked her who or what was crying, and others wanted and demanded to know what was going on. The boy cried louder. Mildred had no alternative. She produced the baby.

Was it hers, they laughed; and who was the father? Which gooseberry bush was to blame? But one woman remarked on its dark skin and screamed: 'It's devil's work!' The crowd recoiled, the children were dragged back by their mothers. Another woman said: 'Baby's hungry, that's all,' and there were crude suggestions that Mildred should give it suck, and so on. Jane Stone, wife of Silas, appeared on the scene and imposed order.

'Mildred Skinner, tell me how you came by the child,' she said.

'He's mine,' Mildred replied, flashing her fierce eyes.

'Did you steal him?'

'Saved him.'

'Where was that?'

'Yonder – left to die.'

'Is that true?'

'It is.'

'You'd better give him to a woman to look after, then we'll talk to Silas.'

'I'm giving him to nobody.'

'But you've had no children. How do you think you'll feed him?'

'Leave me be!'

'He'll die, Mildred, without food.'

'I'll get milk from Nanny Herder.'

Joe Herder kept goats and his wife Anne was nicknamed Nanny because of them – she also looked like a goat.

Jane Stone said: 'Well, we'll see. But I hope the boy lives till Silas can decide what ought to be done.'

Mildred had returned the bellowing babe to her bag, and now drew her axe and waved it at the people.

'Get away from me,' she shouted at them.

The crowd muttered and dispersed, shaking fists and heads.

Mildred obtained some goat's milk in exchange for watercress. Nanny Herder poured some down the baby's throat, and squirted some out of an old pig's bladder. She had raised four sons and a daughter, and fed innumerable kids – baby goats – by hand. She would be described as a 'motherly' woman by today's sentimentalists. She was not so squeamish as her husband Michael and slaughtered their goats without compunction.

'He'll be wanting more nourishment in an hour or two,' Nanny said.

'I know,' Mildred lied in reply.

'Where are you going to get it from?'

'I'll have more of your goat's milk.'

'Will you now!'

'I'll give you cress for it.'

'That's more like it. He'll need washing after he's fed.'

'I know.'

'That you don't! I've had five children. I'll take care of baby if you'll keep me in watercress.'

'Four of your children died.'

'Oh you spiteful woman! No wonder no man would touch you. Where's the cress for the milk you're wanting?'

The exchange took place.

Mildred carried the baby upstream to wash him and was cursed by the women downstream fetching water for drinking and cooking – they said she was trying to make them sick.

The women of Woody were angry with Mildred for having a baby without tears or suffering. They were united against her and hung about, waiting to scream their objections at Silas.

He returned from the forest at dusk. He was greeted by his wife Jane and a mob of twenty or so other wives and mothers. He approached Mildred.

'What's this I hear?' he asked straight out in his deep voice, smiling in a friendly way.

'Mind your business,' she retorted.

'You've brought a baby home, haven't you?'

'Why ask if you know?'

'I'll thank you to keep a civil tongue in your head.'

'And I'll thank you to go away.'

'That I won't. Whose baby is it, Mildred? Did you steal it?'

'No.'

'What then?'

'Found it.'

'Where?'

She gestured towards the forest.

'Would you call it a foundling?'

She shrugged her shoulders.

'Show it to me, please.'

She went indoors and reappeared with the foundling in her arms.

'It's a boy,' she volunteered.

'It's not long born. We better get it christened in case it dies and goes down below.'

'I don't hold with that.'

'Makes no difference what you hold with. We're not having a heathen here in Woody. What's his name?'

'He's got nothing.'

'We'll call him Theodore. That means given by God.'

'Please yourself.'

'Theodore Widdle.'

'Theodore Skinner,' she insisted.

'Look, he can't be Skinner. You were a married Widdle, and Widdle he'll be. We'll wheel you to the Vicarage in Gorham in the morning, you and the foundling. I'll speak for you, and be sure he'll live and die a Widdle.'

'He won't die.'

'Course he will if you try to mother him. Give him to one of these women – they've enough milk to feed another mouth.'

He pointed at two heavy-breasted members of the mob, a scowler who turned her back on him, and a giggler with a child at foot.

Silas said to the latter: 'You'll feed another baby, won't you, Esther? You could feed half a dozen more, I dare say.'

General laughter greeted this sally, and Mildred retreated towards the open doorway of her dwelling.

'Here,' Silas addressed her, 'Where d'you think you're going? We'll have that baby off you, then you can do what you like. Hand him over, Mildred!'

'I won't.'

'Think it over, any rate. We don't want un-pleasantness. You'll see that baby dying shortly, because it will without proper feeding, and you'll cry out for help. Mark my words!'

'Go to hell!'

'I heard that, Mildred, you bitter old booby. Tell you what – we'll be taking your baby soon as I've had my victuals – and no nonsense, mind!'

Silas shooed the mob away, and went home with Jane.

Mildred, indoors, in the darkening gloom of her living room, spoke to the baby.

'It wasn't God that gave you to me, not Him – could be the other one. Foundling they call you – changeling, more like, bad fairies' boy. Don't you look at me – I'm not fighting for you, I'm not! They can have you for all I care. Where's that milk? You drink this, boy, or else!'

She crumpled a leaf into a funnel, forced it between the baby's lips, channelled some of the milk into him, and changed her mind.

'You'll be Maisie's some time never. And I won't let you be a Widdle. Those jealous cats, they'll steal you for their own. What's to be done, my headache?'

She rocked the baby in her arms and said: 'You're better than nothing, I may agree. You don't make a fuss, I will say in your favour. Shall we elope, child? No good will come to you or me in this place. And summer's near and warm weather.'

Night had fallen. The moon shone. Mildred

munched bread and watercress, and the baby slept.

Then in a hurry she bundled clothing and pieces of fur into a sack with the remains of food. She replaced the baby in her bag and slung the bag over her shoulders, took her thumbstick, and stealthily at first, then as fast as she could walk, she returned to the farther unfrequented acreage of the forest.

Against even her own expectations they survived that summer and winter, and several more seasons. She stole milk from cows in fields and food from kitchens and middens, and they slept in the open or in old hollow trees. But they were often starving, and life was always precarious.

The First Rung

Soon after dawn on a raw autumn morning a score or so of foresters sallied forth from Wood Houses and plodded into the Forest. The man in front was Jonathan Stone, son of the late Silas, now nearly thirty and with grey in his beard. All the men wore over-garments to keep out the cold and wet, cloaks with cowls, shawls round shoulders; and they were careful not to expose their axes and saws to the rain.

Moribund leaves dangled on the branches of trees, and the fallen leaves were losing their rich orange colour and turning into squelchiness underfoot. The only birdsong was the cawing of crows in the distance. Some of the men talked together in voices lowered on account of the depressing weather.

They arrived at the part of the forest where they had worked for several days. It was at the farther end of the woodland thought to belong to Squire Dunbee. The men divested themselves of clothes that would get in the way of their work and hung them from the twigs of trees; while a youth called Simon tried to get a bonfire going nearby which would keep the clothing as dry as possible – Simon had brought kindling with him. Axes were produced, the sharpness of blades tested against thumbs, the palms of hands spat upon, and the chopping began.

Immediately a loud cry from Simon interrupted the proceedings.

'Looky here!' he cried out, and the men called back, 'What's up? What's wrong?'

Simon was pointing at something under a bush. The men approached and peered where Simon pointed. Two large brown eyes stared at them without blinking. They thought it was an animal – they said so, and some of them recoiled.

Negatives, 'No – no – not that – nay – never,' were followed by a positive exclamation: 'It's a 'uman!'

Somebody reached in and pulled out a boy of two or three, stunted, weighing too little, with hollow cheeks, a neck like a pipe and a swollen belly. He was filthy, dirty-faced with long, tangled, blackish hair on his head – he had hair on his arms and legs, too – and was naked except for a cloth in tatters fastened with a knot across his chest. He could not stand up, he toppled over and measured his length on the wet ground. He was passive and silent: only his brown eyes showed he was alive.

He inspired more fear than pity. The man who had pulled him into the light of day said his arms were like icicles. Another man asked suspiciously: 'What's he doing here?' A third invoked the devil, and a fourth said he was an elf. 'Don't you touch him,' they warned Jonathan

Stone, who was taking charge in the manner of his forebears.

Jonathan produced the green bottle strapped to his belt – it contained water flavoured with honey and warmed by his body – and managed to pour some of the liquid into the boy's mouth. It was swallowed. The boy swallowed more of the sweet lukewarm mixture. Jonathan tried him with a corner of hand-baked bread. The boy chewed it and summoned the ghost of a smile.

'I know you,' Jonathan said, and, turning to the assembled company, he explained: 'This is the boy Mildred Widdle as was Skinner found. He's Theodore Widdle who never was christened. She ran off with him into the woods.'

'Aye – so it is – you're right there, I shouldn't wonder – well spotted, Jonathan,' the older foresters agreed. But Amos, who was mean-minded as well as old, spoke up: 'He was devil's spawn then and he's devil's spawn now.'

Jonathan replied: 'We'll take him to church for baptising, and that'll show if he's anything to do with Old Nick. You hold off, Amos, till the Almighty's had his chance to tell us true. I'll carry the lad home and let the women see how much life's in him. He'll die for sure otherwise, and I'd like to have the harm drawn out of him, if any. You carry on, and I'll be back soon as maybe.'

At Woody, Jonathan summoned his wife Sue and his mother Jane, and, in front of the crowd of villagers that also gathered, he handed over Theodore.

Doubts were again aired. Theodore was touched and prodded by other children, and grown-ups asked personal questions and passed hostile remarks.

'Can you talk, boy? ... Why are you so thin? ... Why so mucky? ... He's got a big belly, he must have eaten a lot ... I don't want him mixing with mine ... He's sick, you can see it ... He's evil.'

Jonathan returned to the place where he had left his workmates.

He said to them: 'My mother and my Sue recognised that there Theodore. Mildred Widdle as was Skinner must have kept him going this long time. She'll be about somewhere, and I'm tempted to look for her and give her a decent burial, poor soul, though she was a bitch while she lived.'

The men were agreed, and began to search. They did not have to search far. Mildred lay in the open, on a patch of green sward, where she must have fallen and expired; it was some twenty yards beyond the bush Theodore had crept under. She was almost a skeleton, and the magpies had stolen her eyes.

They buried her bones. Again, those who remembered her would have left her to rot, and others were against getting involved in still more business that was possibly fateful. But they were all swayed by the idea that if she was not underground she would be eaten by foxes.

Jonathan, back at Woody, received a scratchy welcome from Sue. In their living room, Theodore slept on a mat on the floor. Three little Stones, Jonathan's offspring, sat in a row on a bench, staring at the intruder, and Sue demanded to know what she was meant to do next.

'Have you fed him?' Jonathan inquired.

'I have, and I'm sorry – he'll eat me out of house and home,' she replied. 'I'm not letting our boys go short because of a stranger, that's my last word, Jonathan. And he's crawling and he stinks.'

'He'll get a scrubbing tomorrow, and I'll hack away his hair.'

Seven-year-old Dan Stone remarked: 'He's got hair all over.'

'So would you have if you'd lived out in the cold in winter,' Jonathan informed him.

Sue returned to the charge.

'What then, Jonathan? I'm not slaving for him, mind.'

'I'll have him christened tomorrow.'

'But afterwards? It's all very well to make a Christian of him. What I'm telling you is that I've got enough Christians to see to.'

'Steady, my dear.'

'Your mother agrees with me. She says I'm not to put up with him any longer.'

'Well, that's my thought, too, if you want to know. He won't last long after what he's been through. I give him a couple of days, no more. So where's my supper?'

Years passed, fifteen and more years. The forest still grew up and was cut down, and remained

25

more or less the same. Something similar applied in the human context. Five members of the Stone family were dead: Jane, widow of Silas, Jonathan, Silas's son, Sue his wife, and their sons Matthew and Mark. The two foresters Amos and Simon were underground, but other men swung their axes. And Dan Stone, another casualty of the pestilence, lingering between life and death, was now the husband of Martha and the father of four children.

Theodore Widdle still lived with the Stones. Jonathan Stone's Sue had lost the battle to exclude him from her home. He earned his keep from an early age, working with the foresters, collecting wood chippings and sawdust. When he was older, he rendered services during the period of sickness and bereavement in the whole community of Wood Houses. Dan and Martha continued to feed him by way of thanks for his kind acts and nursing, and they let him sleep in an outhouse.

Theodore grew to be as strong as he had been weak once upon a time. At sixteen he was able to take turns with axes and with the dummer. Then the Stones gave him the saw that had belonged to Silas, and at seventeen he could do more than a full day's work, for he was tireless and inclined to skip rest periods.

He was never a sociable type. He was silent and wary from the start. He watched grown-ups – he seemed to be studying and judging them, and was often ordered not to stare. He did not play with other boys voluntarily – perhaps they had been told to keep their distance from the unaccountable stranger – but he would join in races if asked to, and usually win them. He received scant education, yet was bookish, sometimes allowed to borrow the Stones' family Bible for an hour or two, and would pore over it in the light summer evenings. That he should be sent to sleep in an outhouse, like a dog to its kennel, caused him no visible concern – he kept his bed, and himself for that matter, clean, and privacy somehow suited him.

Theodore was altogether different from the youths of Wood Houses. His strength was not in bulging muscles or bulk, he was slender and lithe. He was not fair in any respect, his hair was black and curly, his complexion brownish, his eyes dark brown, and his teeth shiny white and not yet showing signs of decay. Rumours were that he was a Romany, even though Romanys were noted for their kindness to children – they were unlikely to have left a baby to die in a sack. He could have been foreign, people said, and were not argued with, for no one in Wood Houses had ever seen a foreigner.

His uniqueness combined with his physical attributes found favour with the opposite sex. Little girls had cuddled him, and now bigger girls hoped he would do the cuddling. They were disappointed: again he was unwilling to play, and the Commandments of God were adhered to at Wood Houses. Fear of the fires of hell instilled chastity and discipline, and the lusts of the flesh were controlled to the best of everybody's ability. Martha Stone's relationship with Theodore was strictly platonic in spite of her occasional sighs when he retired to his outhouse of an evening. A few girls dared to smile at him, and reckless ones ogled him in church. He took no notice, although they knew, as women always do, that he was far from impervious to their charms.

His own sex tolerated him, in the beginning he was spared by incomprehension and superstition, and now he was respected.

Needless to say, in the countryside where the daily round was grim and boring, and a good story was a change equal to a holiday, the fate of the little boy who had escaped death twice over was discussed widely. An abandoned baby might be humdrum entertainment, but such a baby rescued against the odds by accident, and then surviving a spell in the forest with a witch, was sensational. Squire Dunbee had eventually heard tell of Theodore, and one day in Wood Houses asked Jonathan Stone to point him out.

'Where's his fur?' the Squire demanded.

Jonathan said that he had lost the hair on his body since he wore clothes and was sheltered from the cold weather.

Squire was clearly disappointed, and voiced the single comment: 'Well – he don't look English.'

However, after a gap of nearly a decade, Squire Dunbee again referred to Theodore. He rode into Wood Houses to collect his rent, followed by his agent Yates, and a young woman, also on horseback. The Squire dismounted. Yates followed suit and assisted the girl on to the ground. Dan, Jonathan's son, appeared together with two men, foresters, who ran forward to hold on to the bridles of the horses. Dan saluted and bowed, handed over a leathern bag of money, as was customary, and, after a few polite exchanges, was asked by the Squire: 'That peculiar boy alive?'

'Which one would that be, sir?'

'The boy who lived in the forest, he had a funny name.'

'Theodore Widdle, sir?'

'That's him.'

'He is, sir, alive and kicking.'

'Is he about?'

'He's sharpening saws in my house, sir – he lives in our house.'

'Fetch him, will you? I'd like to have a look at what he's growed into.'

Dan did as he was told, and Theodore emerged through the Stones' dark doorway, shielding his eyes against the bright light.

'Are you Widdle?' Squire Dunbee called out.

'Yes, sir.'

'Morning, morning!'

Theodore responded with a deferential sort of bow.

The Squire turned to the girl and questioned: 'Is that what you wanted?'

Dan saluted her with his hand, his version of 'pulling his forelock', and he and Theodore chorused: 'Morning, Miss.'

Squire Dunbee addressed his daughter as if to scold her; 'Come along, Ann.'

He approached his horse, a cob with docked tail. He held the reins with one hand and the saddle with the other, and Yates stepped forward to give him a leg up, cupping hands to hold Squire's foot and enabling him to swing his other leg over the horse's back and to settle into the saddle.

Miss Dunbee's horse was led forward. But it was fresh, danced away, and she needed help to mount into her oddly shaped saddle – it was designed for ladies riding side-saddle, especially for girls, who were thought to break their hymens by riding with legs astride. Again Yates stepped forward, but she waved him away with an irritable gesture.

She summoned Widdle by his surname – it was an order.

'Bend down and hold my foot!' she said.

He did so without a word.

'Lift me up,' she commanded.

She had her foot in Theodore's hands, but he must have lifted with more force than expected, for she toppled unsteadily. To stop her falling, he removed one hand from her foot and placed it on her lower back. She reached her saddle, showing sudden spots of colour in her cheeks. She hooked her right leg over the protrusion and, sitting sideways, arranged the skirt so that it hid her legs.

She scowled down at him and said, 'Clumsy fool!'

*   *   *

After the Dunbee cavalcade had gone, Dan said to Theodore: 'I think she's sweet on you.'

Theodore shrugged his shoulders and returned to his task of filing the teeth of saws belonging to himself and other foresters.

That Sunday in Gorham Church he was aware of Ann Dunbee's eyes resting on him, or, rather, drilling into him. He had been aware of her presence in church for several years. The Dunbees were the gentry of Gorham, and they had paid to have pews for their family in a side chapel. Ann sat in the front pew on one side of her father, the red-faced Squire, who had Mrs Dunbee on his other side, a wilting scrap of a woman, exhausted by having borne five children for her husband. Ann was the eldest, and the only girl. She was twenty-five years old and in danger of becoming her father's housekeeper and factotum since her mother ailed. The four sons ranged in age from twenty-one to seventeen. The eldest was married but had as yet produced no issue. The other three were unmarried. They all, together with the grandparents, an uncle, aunts and cousins, filled the rest of the spaces in the pews.

Ann was not beautiful. She bore a resemblance to a white mouse. It was the colourlessness of her skin, and her hair which was so blond and fine as to be scarcely visible, that suggested the likeness. Her dark blue eyes were not in harmony with the rest of her face – they clashed with her pallor. They also smouldered – they were like hot coals in snow. And then her nose was beaky and her lips were thin. Her figure was her redeeming feature: it was womanly and still trim.

Several weeks passed, marked for Theodore by the irreligious stares of Ann Dunbee on Sunday mornings. She left the church with her family before the rest of the congregation: he never saw her elsewhere.

Then, apparently, she rode through Wood Houses one afternoon. Martha Stone told Theodore she was sure Miss Ann had been looking for him. Theodore denied it; but there were jokes and teasing. Martha said he was too young to take on a madam so long in the tooth, and Dan that she would have him in the end. It was all fanciful stuff – none of them believed a match could ever be made.

The disaster that struck the Dunbees exerted influence of another sort. An ague, a murrain possibly connected with agriculture, struck down Ann's mother and her three brothers and her sister-in-law. The departed were well and in church on one Sunday, in the next they were being prayed for, and in the one after that they were mourned.

Ann attended those services. In the second she stared at Theodore with an unfathomable expression, and in the third she did her staring through a veil.

After the funerals she underwent an obvious change. It was not grief, it was not quite decent. She marched into the family pew on Sundays in her black clothing as if with flags flying. She dragged her stricken father in and out with impatience. She almost tossed her head at Theodore.

Shortly afterwards, on a warm morning in the month of May, he was sent to gather the fallen 'needles' of the yew trees that grew in a far part of the Forest. These 'needles', no longer evergreen but brown, were packed in sacks by the foresters and sold as palliasses – they were softer than straw to sleep on. While he bent to the work he heard the sound of a horse walking along a nearby ride, one of the many passable forest tracks. It stopped – it must have been twenty yards distant – and he vaguely heard someone dismount and then sounds of the horse cropping the grass and tender shoots.

He straightened up and was startled to see Ann Dunbee not much more than ten yards away, squatting to answer a call of nature. There was nothing immodest about it – the yew trees cast dark shadow, she was in a sequestered place, and obviously thought she would not be seen. But he was unable to move, also unwilling, in case a movement caught her eye; and she finished, grasped the riding stick or switch that she had laid on the ground, rose to her full height and saw him.

They were both immovable. The stares they were exchanging had a new content. She had the grace to blush – he noticed the unwonted blob of pink in her cheeks. And she was the one to take the initiative. She dropped her skirt which she was holding up with her other hand and slapped the switch against a re-clothed leg angrily.

'You spied on me,' she said in a harsh voice.
'No, Miss –'
'You're insolent.'
'No, Miss.'
'Don't argue with me. Come here!'

He hesitated. He was not prepared to be ordered about. But she might be playing a game. He took a few steps in her direction.

'Drop your breeches!'
'That I won't.'
'Then I'll whip your cheeky face.'
'You shouldn't talk to me like that.'
'Hold your tongue! You've seen too much of me. It's your turn.'

Their eyes locked again, and the queries in his and in hers had the effect of raising their temperatures.

'Do as I say,' she said a bit breathlessly.

He undid the knot in the cord round his waist and his breeches fell to his ankles.

She looked at him and scolded between gasps: 'You bad man ... Disgusting! ... I'll teach you ...' And she raised the switch as if to strike him in a region of his anatomy that was out of bounds.

He stepped closer and caught her wrist. Perhaps she gave him time to catch it. Anyway they were close enough to wrestle, and she fell backwards with him on top of her. They wrestled and squirmed, and somehow or other her skirt and petticoats rode up, and after a few minutes a groan and a squeal caused her horse to whinny and pigeons to take fright and flap out of the high trees.

They rolled apart. They struggled to their feet. She picked up her switch and headed for her horse. He tied his breeches in position and followed her. She unhooked the horse's bridle from the branch and stood by the saddle. She could have mounted without assistance, she had expected to do so, but now she waited, and he took the hint and put his hands round her thighs and lifted her up. She arranged herself and propelled the horse forwards. Fifty or so yards down the track she turned her almost white head and gazed back at Theodore, who had stayed put and now watched her out of sight.

Days passed, and weeks, and three months. He lived in terror of unimaginable repercussions. She had appeared in church on the Sunday after the episode under the yews; but she had not looked at him once, and since then had not shown her face anywhere. He gradually ceased to dread revenge, and to indulge in speculation that was part hope that they would get together again and part hope that they would not.

In August Squire Dunbee came to Wood Houses not to collect his rent – an exceptional occasion. He was driven over in an ancient horse-drawn vehicle: since the loss of his wife and sons he had aged and no longer rode his cob. It was afternoon, the foresters were returning home, and the Squire gave the order that he wished to speak to Theodore Widdle.

Theodore reported in due course, apologised for his working clothes, was told to climb into the type of wagon known locally as a wain, and stood on the flat floorboards in front of the old man, who was seated, purple in the face, eyeing him murderously, and spoke to him between gasps for breath.

'You have given my daughter a fat belly. I will not be the grandfather of a bastard, and my daughter is determined that you shall make an honest woman of her. She is wilful, and has turned her nose up at better men than you are. I disapprove of everything you and she have done, and most of all I disapprove of a Dunbee marrying a foundling and a nobody. I am blunt, sir, but you must learn to bear my bluntness. The banns of your marriage to my daughter will be read for the first time next Sunday, and the wedding will take place as soon as the vicar can do the job. Ann is moneyed and has expectations, but should you steal from her I'll have you hanged if I'm alive and shall haunt you if I'm dead. My agent Yates will see that you have a decent suit to be married in. You and Ann will live with me at Dunbee Court after you are man and wife. Now get out of my sight.'

More surprises were in store for Theodore. His surname, pronounced from the pulpit in Gorham Church, had been changed to Widell; and Widell was spoken with the emphasis on the second syllable.

Ann had reappeared in the family pew to hear the banns read; and she and Theodore exchanged glances; but the messages in their eyes were not clear, and after the service she was whisked back to Dunbee Court by the Squire, while Theodore legged it to Wood Houses.

He had a lot to put up with. He did not like to be treated with disdain by the Dunbees. He was embarrassed by having to confess to his workmates and neighbours that he scarcely knew his future wife and that his future father-in-law had threatened to hang him. He was accused by his contempories of marrying for money, and in order to pull rank on humble folk. Mr Yates, the Squire's oily and resentful man of business, jeered at him for not knowing how to tie a neckerchief and which buttons on his wedding waistcoat he was to do up and to leave undone. Not the least bad consequence of his engagement were the rustic jokes and occasional compliments directed at his nether region.

On the other hand, he was willing. He could recognise luck when he saw it. At the altar in St Mary's church in Gorham, he uttered his vows with audible conviction.

In the night after the wedding he was surprised twice. His wife had starved for so long that he had to work hard to satisfy her carnal appetite. And in a brief break from bodily worship she said to him: 'I won't have you dirtying your hands with labourer's work. I mean to teach you to deserve me.'

The practical application of Ann's theory was that she began to teach him his ABC, how to write his new name, spelling, sums, also etiquette, manners, polite conversation and social niceties.

She set him homework. She kept his nose to every sort of grindstone. She punished him with the sharpness of her tongue and even dared to slap him.

They lived in Dunbee Court, and ate at Squire Dunbee's table. He too dinned information into Theodore's head. He wanted his ill-bred ignorant orphan of a son-in-law to know that the blood in the veins of his child on the way was ancient and damn nearly blue. He said that he and his forefathers always were the kings of Gorham, and should have been crowned formally years ago. Theodore was never to forget how privileged he was to have gained entry into such an illustrious family by the tradesmen's door, not to mince matters. Moreover, neither Widell should forget, the Squire rumbled in his cups, that all they would gain from his death was snatched from the hands of his three dear and irreplaceable sons.

Theodore attended closely to these boasts and insults. Should he show inattention, he would be rebuked in disagreeable terms: 'Yawn at me, sir, I'll wake you with the toe of my boot ... Listen and learn, boy – any fool can please a woman!'

In fact Theodore learned fast. He saw the point of Ann's lessons, and was all ears when she and her father discussed property and money. The wealth of the Dunbees exceeded his fanciful estimates, and inspired him by opening up prospects of power. But he was reserved by nature, and had the nous to be discreet. He bit his tongue and did his marital duty – Ann had no cause to complain.

The baby was a boy, christened Benjamin because he was born fortunate, and Dunbee for obvious reasons – Benjamin Dunbee Widell.

Ann was pregnant again with minimum delay, and in the next two years Prudence Widell and Edward Widell joined Ben in the nursery quarters of Dunbee Court.

Then the Squire went to meet his Maker. He was drunk at the time, and in irascible mood, and cursed himself into a fatal seizure.

After the period of mourning had elapsed, in the withdrawing room of Dunbee Court on a chill spring evening, an exceptional scene was played out. Theodore and Ann had eaten their evening meal. He stood in front of the fire of logs supplied by the foresters of Wood Houses, she sewed special garments for their children. He was changed for the better by matrimony and time, he had filled out and looked impressive in his mid-twenties. She was changed for the worse, her hair looked like dry straw, but her eyes were still as sharp as the needle she wielded.

'Ann,' he began.

'What is it?' she asked as if he were interrupting.

'I owe you and your family a debt. I am your husband, your late father's son-in-law, and a man of consequence. Thanks to you, I have received education and discovered the meaning of money. But, as I see it, my apprenticeship has been served, and I am bound to take responsibility for the welfare of our family.'

'What nonsense are you talking, Theodore?'

'I have sacked Yates. He will vacate his cottage tomorrow morning. If he attempts to discuss his dismissal with you, I have warned him that I shall call in the law.'

'Are you mad? Mr Yates has looked after us, after the Dunbees, for years. You have no right to sack him. I shall cancel your order immediately.'

'If you do, he will not only be sacked, he will be sent to prison. He robbed your father, and has robbed you and me, consistently. I have records that he has stolen in excess of twenty thousand pounds.'

'That's a lie.'

'My dear, I give you permission to go to Yates and reinstate him. He will not thank you when he is taken to prison tomorrow.'

'Who has seen these records?'

'Two independent men with heads for figures, the clerk of the council, Mr Withers, and the treasurer of Gorham Church, Mr Appleyard. To continue, Ann: Dan Stone from Woody, with his wife and children, will be moving into Yates' cottage. Dan has been ill for a long time, but has recovered and is well and strong again. He is not a mathematician, but he is honest and true, and, like his father and grandfather, was always my friend. Mathematicians can be hired.'

'I think I'm dreaming, Theodore. You are not authorised to do any of these things. I won't stand for it.'

'My dear, you should have thought of all that before you married me. You gave me authority along with your vows in church. I am not taking advantage of you, I am at last availing myself of the advantages you granted me, forced upon me, with body and soul.'

'Shut your mouth, Theodore! I will not listen to any more of this.'

'Sit down! The door is locked. You will hear me out for a change, as I've heard you until tonight. The Dunbee estate has been mismanaged. Your father was a bad businessman, and Yates has been interested in nothing but feathering his own nest. The remainder of the Forest of Woody and the adjoining farm of five hundred acres have been for sale for eighteen months. Their owner, Squire Kingcomb, has fallen on evil days, and he needs money so badly that he will sell for a song. Meanwhile the Dunbee treasure has been locked away by Yates and subject to embezzlement. Now I have bought both Forest and farm. I have ordered advertisement for more foresters, and for a tenant farmer prepared to pay a modest rent, and commissioned the building of extra accommodation at Wood Houses.'

'Wicked – Father told me not to marry you – you have acted without my permission – wicked, Theodore.'

'Not so, my dear. I have begun to repay my debts. Let me remind you that you are no longer a Dunbee. You are a Widell, and I aim to make you and your children, who are also mine, richer than the Dunbees ever were or would become. We shall be rich and envied. Our descendants will be rich and famous. With that in mind, I have also commissioned an architect to draw plans for a larger, more convenient home to stand on top of the foundations of this old one. It is to be called Widell Manor.'

'To think...' Ann snivelled inconclusively. 'To think...' she repeated and started to cry.

'I'm glad to see your tears,' Theodore observed. 'They show you may become a gentle woman after all. Go to bed! I'll unlock that door, and join you in a while.'

The Touch Of Royalty

Theodore Widell sat at the great mahogany desk in the business room of his manorial residence with his grey head in his hands.

He was old and distressed. He was still fine-looking, brown-eyed, dark-skinned, better dressed than most agriculturalists, and creating an impression of strength at bay. He was inactive in the middle of a summer's morning, which was unusual. He was waiting for his eldest son, his first-born child Benjamin, now in his late thirties, and resolving – or hoping – not to lose his temper and make himself iller than he already feared he was.

Theodore's long list of successes filled page after page of the book of destiny; but each of those pages had its verso, on which was written in large black letters the word Ben.

The boy had been suspect from his earliest days. He bore no resemblance to either his father or his mother: he was red-faced and had carroty-coloured hair. He was rough, he broke his toys and hit his contemporaries, and impenetrably dense. He was greedy beyond pardon, he stole food from his younger siblings, and his mindless good humour did not compensate for his failings.

Ann had retailed news from the nursery to Theodore, and it led to quarrels. Although the shrew was tamed by the forcefulness of her husband and the multiplicity of her children, she could not stop herself complaining of Ben's faults and putting the blame on the heredity of Theodore, who was provoked into pointing out that Ben aged four looked like Squire Dunbee at fifty-four. The senior Widells continued to disagree about Ben as he grew up: he was the blot on their matrimonial landscape, as well as being Theodore's dynastic disappointment and, what with tutoring and then with debts, an open drain for money.

Ben, by accident or design, exemplified the even-handedness of nature. He seemed to be driven to do everything his father had not done and to undo all he had done. He was also as indiscriminate as his mother was exclusive and haughty – he was addicted to the joys of taverns at an early age and made friends with roisterers and hoydens. That he stooped to mix with a woman called Maisie, and that the two of them got engaged to marry in the countrified manner, in other words the family way, struck Ann as a sly and rude reference to her own engagement to Theodore.

Maisie admitting to twenty-nine years of age marrying Ben aged twenty-two was, according to Ann, a baby-snatcher and a gold-digger as well as a slattern and a strumpet. Maisie heard tell, daggers were accordingly drawn, and Ben's wife missed no opportunity to encourage him to annoy his parents. The junior Widells lived in the remnant of Dunbee Court, close to Widell Manor, therefore Theodore and Ann were forced to notice that Ben was not attending to estate work – he was loitering in the vicinity of the stable yard; had bought expensive horses they would have to pay for; was entertaining ribald company night after night; and proving to the whole world – of Gorham and Wood Houses – that he was a wastrel.

Theodore paid Ben for the work he skimped and neglected. But Ben overspent as if on principle. He owed shopkeepers, innkeepers, horse-copers, men he gambled with, even his own servants; and his creditors called at Dunbee Lodge and were screamed at by Maisie for their pains. Ultimately the creditors came to Widell Manor – before long they did not bother with the Lodge and the curses of Mrs Ben Widell in her grubby night attire at midday.

The door of the study burst open – no knock, no respect – and scattered Theodore's thoughts and good intentions.

Ben, ill-dressed, scarlet in the face, grubby, probably tipsy, stood on the other side of the desk.

'Morning,' he shouted.

'I've a letter here from Farmer Jenkinson,' Theodore replied. 'He's telling me he won the Forest of Woody playing cards with you.'

'I might have won Jenkinson's farm, Father.'

'But you lost.'

'Did I, by Jove?'

'Don't you know if you lost or won?'

'Steady, Father – it's only trees.'

Theodore, almost visibly grinding his teeth, stared at his son.

Ben looked scared and began: 'I say—'

But Theodore interrupted: 'No – you'll say no more – you'll listen. You gambled with Farmer Jenkinson and lost our Forest, now Farmer Jenkinson offers to sell our Forest back to me. I'm accepting the offer – it will cost me dear – so you'll get not a penny more from me, never one penny. And I'll be evicting you from Dunbee Lodge – I want a tenant there who pays me.'

'Where do I live, Father – me and Maisie and George? George is your grandson.'

'Maybe so – maybe you are my son – but you're not my heir – I've cut you out of my will.'

'I say, that's steep.'

'Leave my house!'

'Where's Ma?'

'Did you hear me, Ben?'

'Ma won't let you roast me.'

'Wrong again – you always have been wrong – you always will be wrong. Leave my house before I ring for the servants.'

'Wait till Maisie hears.'

'Out, out!'

Ben slouched off as instructed.

Theodore grimaced with pain and placed one shaky hand on his chest, and with the other rang a silver handbell on his desk.

To the serving-man who responded he said: 'Fetch my wife.'

* * *

Soon after the death of Theodore Widell, an epidemic that might have been a precursor of the Great Plague of 1665 carried off his widow and three of his daughters.

Theodore's second son, Edward, together with wife Harriet and two boys, James and Gregory, moved into Widell Manor.

Ben disappeared; but some years later Maisie Widell turned up in Bushton. She let on that her husband had drowned in a ditch, and George had perished somehow or other. She vowed she was going to get money out of the Widells. She approached Edward, who had her put in prison for threatening to castrate him. She then removed herself or was removed from the area.

Edward had created a business that made money in lean and in fat years. He was an undertaker. He had coffins knocked together in Wood Houses by the men who cut the trees and sawed the planks that were now part of his own inheritance.

In the front parlour of his commercial premises he had extracted money from the bereaved with his obsequious sympathy, that tool of his trade, and his efficiency. He carried efficiency to extremes in the back room, where he had been known to remove feet in order to fit a corpse into a coffin. He ceased to handle dead customers after coming into the Widell inheritance. He was a pale neat man, not so pale as his mother Ann, and with nothing of his father showing in his person or personality. Theodore had not liked him; but he had disliked him less than he disliked Ben, and grudgingly admired his mercantile record. Edward's wife Harriet seemed to share her father-in-law's opinions – she behaved as if she felt that Edward could have been worse. Their sons had the looks of future undertakers.

The faint phrase that could be applied to Edward's reign as head of the family was that he neither added one penny nor subtracted one from the fortunes of the Widells. His end was premature even judged by the low life-expectancy criteria then in force. In his thirties he fell from his horse, broke bones, contracted a multiplicity of the diseases recognised by contemporary science, lung fever, putrifying of the extremities, blood on the brain and sclerotic failure of the heart, and not surprisingly breathed his last.

His elder son, James Widell, fared even less well, if possible. He lived to marry and sire a son, Hector; but following his premature demise he was found to have ingested a tapeworm, which had grown and gradually eaten him from the inside out – the discovery was made just before the interment, one of his employees in the undertaker's shop heard movement within the casket.

Hector was slow to talk, let alone read and write. On the other hand he had a sunny nature: it was rumoured that it became sunny when he grasped the fact that he had great expectations. He was foolish and a turnip, but he introduced a novel genetic strand into the heredity of the

Widells: loveability. The Dunbees were never loveable. Theodore, the foundling, had looks and brains, but he was not cosy. Hector was popular with his servants and playmates. Grown-ups found he had a touch of charm. He laughed at other people's jokes after taking his time to see that they were funny.

Throughout Hector's youth Civil War raged in the country, then politicians cut off the head of the King of England. The bad news reached Widell Manor late, and did not affect the life-style of the young master, nor, for that matter, of most of his neighbours. But a widow arrived in Gorham with terrible tales to tell. Her name was Alice Wilby. She had come to Gorham to live in the house of her aunt, recently deceased. She was pretty, black-haired, unencumbered by children, and twentyish, not many years older than Hector. How different her experience had been! Her husband had gone to fight against the upstart Cromwell and for King Charles, he fought for the Cavaliers, was sorely wounded, recovered, contracted the plague of plagues and died of it. And not long ago their house in London, her home, had burned down in the Great Fire. She said how lucky she was to have her Aunt Betty's sweet tiny dwelling in which to try to recover from the blows of fate. She also let it be known that she was impoverished.

Her looks and her predicament, her ladylike manners, and the pity she evoked at least in the hearts of men, drew her into the highest society of the township. She attended the Mayor's functions and the entertainments in the homes of the dozen or so leading citizens. She met Hector everywhere, not only at Widell Manor. Of course the womenfolk noticed that she was setting her cap at him: the wives were relieved, several maidens were disappointed, but one or two wondered whether Alice would be able to bring Hector to the boil, especially considering the nickname applied to her in some quarters, Ice.

Alice shed her mourning garments. She donned colours as bright as she was. She fluttered her eyelids with the dark lashes at Hector. She shook his large hand in her hot, soft, little one longer than was customary. She congratulated him for airing an opinion or essaying a mild pleasantry with a pat or a gentle pinch. She succeeded in separating him from the rest of an assembled company, insisting that she must show him a particular flower at a garden party, or begging for his advice about a minor architectural matter at a musical soirée. As a last resort she took him for a walk along a secluded path in the garden of the Mayor, tripped, fell to the ground, stood close to Hector when he pulled her to her feet and pointed out the mud on a part of her dress above the knee. In vain! Hector said he would get a servant to brush her dress.

His only signal that he was excited by her tricks was his even louder laughter. He admired her, but his admiration took the form of asexual exclamations, for instance: 'What a capital lady you are! What fun we do have together!'

She decided to have recourse to brass tacks.

Subtle hints and invitations had wasted time, and brass was the object of the exercise after all. At some gathering, in exclusive conversation with Hector, she said with a sob that she was too embarrassed to give a party in his honour and show her appreciation of his friendship.

'Oh,' he responded; 'please now – don't you be embarrassed – I'm the embarrassed one – ha ha – there there!'

'I meant embarrassed financially.'

'Oh – that – that's too bad – we'll have to see about that – don't you fret!'

'Can I talk to you, Mr Widell?'

'What? You can indeed. Fire away!'

'Not here.'

'What, what?'

'Would you call on me?'

'I certainly would, at your pleasure – and at mine, good gracious!'

'Tomorrow, eleven in the morning?'

'On the dot!'

He duly knocked on the door of her cottage. She did not hurry to let him in, she was not averse to their being coupled together by gossip. They had to sit rather close together on the settee in her sitting-room. Hector was clearly excited by her proximity, he was perspiring and his eyes seemed to roll around in their sockets.

'What's all this?' he asked. 'I don't like to see you in a fuss.'

'How kind you are! I know I can trust you with my secrets. Mr Widell, through no fault of my own I am a poor woman.'

51

'Oh dear – poor! – you've had a drubbing, that I do know – no wonder you're sorry for yourself.'

'I mean I am threatened with poverty.'

'Poverty! Good gracious! Is it money you're short of?'

'How perceptive you are!'

'Poverty, by Jove! So sorry – we can't have that. Look here, may I advance you a little of the needful?'

She uttered a tiny scream of gratitude or impatience and turned her head so that it nuzzled him in the whereabouts of his neck below the jawline.

'Now, now,' he mumbled to comfort or stop her crying, and then found his lips not far from hers. Their lips touched – which of them made the crucial overture? He panted out another of his double-barrelled exclamations, 'I say, I say,' and she threw her arms round his neck and was kissing him like mad.

They broke apart. She pushed him away.

'Forgive me,' she said with a beseeching look. 'I forgot myself. You made me lose my head. Thank you for your generous offer. Alas, you know I am not in a position to accept it.'

'Mrs Wilby,' he began, reaching for a handkerchief with which to mop his brow; 'or may I call you Alice? You must call me Hector now. Well, listen, I would dearly like to ease your monetary predicament, and can see no difficulties for either of us.'

'Dear Hector! You are a man, a wealthy and

powerful man, and I am a weak and lonely woman. If you look again, you will see that I do not have the right to accept your money. I am so sad that I must decline – I wish it was otherwise. But the world would call me a beggar, and worse than a beggar, if I was revealed to have given kisses for cash.'

'It wasn't like that, Alice – dear me, not a bit of it.'

'I hope not. What else could the world think?'

'They could think I was fond of you, that's what, and that's that.'

'Oh Hector, what are you telling me? What are you asking me?'

'I want you ... I want you to take as much of my money as you want.'

'Are you proposing to marry me?'

'What? Very well, yes, why not? You marry me, my dear, that'll put things to rights.'

Tears flowed and lent savour to their kisses.

Soon, perhaps sooner than was suitable in the circumstances, Alice Wilby spoke to Hector Widell thus: 'You have made me happy, and I will make you happy to the best of my ability. We will have fine children. And I am determined, and already have plans, to bring glory in place of a dowry to your name that will be mine. Shall we go to talk to the vicar, dearest?'

But the fine children missed their cue.

Alice Widell controlled her husband in all respects except one: in a sexual context, he was all over the shop. He was too enthusiastic, premature, and then sleepy. To put it another way, he was insufficiently sensual, sensitive, unselfish, patient, knowledgeable, ready to learn from mistakes, or basically interested in the whole business. The consequence was that she grew frustrated, and irritated too, not least by his blissful ignorance. He paid her clumsy compliments – 'My Alice is a blood orange and no mistake ... Best thing I ever did was to bed you, and cheap at the price!' – while she teetered on the brink of ordering him to shut up and learn the lesson of love.

The ladies of Gorham were not slow to remark on the childlessness of the Widells. Widows who had proofs of their fertility were convinced that they could have done better than Alice, a pushy cat if ever there was one, and the virgins blamed Alice for robbing one of them of the chance to present Hector with a son and heir with minimum trouble or delay.

Alice was well aware of the undercurrent of spite. She had to take some of the blame, since Hector had been known to hit the target in the person of a milkmaid in Bushton, who had produced twins; and there was no denying that she had failed to conceive a little Wilby. But she was not lacking in confidence and willpower. She made up her mind to repair the omission and possibly profit into the bargain.

One evening after supper she asked her husband: 'Are you awake, dear?'

'What's that?'

'Are you awake?'

'I wasn't asleep.'

'Of course not. But are you ready to discuss an important matter?'

'Oh – discuss – that's different – it's late in the day for discussion – better not disturb our stomachs after we've eaten hearty. Ha ha!'

'I'm not joking, dear.'

'Oh Lord!'

'I need to see a doctor for your sake, Hector – a doctor in London who will help me to give you a son and other children.'

'What sort of doctor is that? He must be a blackguard.'

'He's a doctor for women, he only gives women pills.'

'I'm not having him give you anything else. Why not have a chat with Dr Pennyfeather here in Gorham?'

'I couldn't, Hector. Dr Pennyfeather dines with us. I couldn't whisper my secrets and yours into his deaf old ear.'

'True, true! But London, dear! I can't recall any member of my family ever going to London. It's a long way off, you know.'

'I do know that, and I know you'll be kind to me as you always are. And you'll forgive me for longing to be the mother of your children. I'm going next Wednesday and will stay with my friends in London, the Westingtons, who are well-connected people.'

'Wednesday, is it? I shall be dull without you, my pet. What will I find to do?'

'You'll behave yourself, and I'll be home soon and promise to make up for lost time, if you understand me, sir.'

'Is that so? You saucy vixen! Wednesday you're going? I'll make a note of that.'

Alice put her plan into action. In London, in the house of the Westingtons in Hillaby Square, she sought the assistance of her girlhood friend Ella, now a woman of fashion, as they plied their needles one afternoon.

'You have wondered what brings such a bumpkin to London,' she began. 'I have come to renew our precious friendship, and you have reassured me with your hospitality and affection that all is as it used to be between us. But I do have a confession to make. My husband is the best man in the world, naturally, but, as you will not be surprised to hear, he has his limits. His wish is to make more of a mark upon history than he is likely to by virtue of his talent or merit. He has therefore hit on the idea of "courting" success in the old-established manner. A very fine gentleman, the finest in the land, is due to tour our part of the country in the near future. You will have heard of it? Yes, the tour is designed to give the people a chance to celebrate his restoration to the throne of his forefathers. My Hector desires him to visit Gorham and spend the night at Widell Manor. I must confess that I am here with you in hopes of pursuing that aim. Are you still acquainted with His Majesty's Private Secretary, Ella, my dear?'

Mrs Westington murmured an affirmative. She was not enchanted by the turn of their talk. She had had private dealings with the Private Secretary in question, Sir Wilson Broadbent. During the Great Fire, Desmond Westington had offered Sir Wilson, who had lost his home in the conflagration, shelter in Hillaby Square. And Ella had confided in her friend Alice that he had often attempted to take advantage of her husband's charitable impulse. Now, her betrayal of the fact that she would have preferred not to discuss Sir Wilson confirmed Alice's suspicions that his attempts had met with some success, and Ella would be easier to manipulate than would have been the case if she had been wholly innocent.

'I need to meet with Sir Wilson,' Alice said. 'I have a letter from Hector to His Majesty with me, an invitation to visit us, and Sir Wilson would be the ideal person to carry it to its destination and make certain that it is read. Would you invite Sir Wilson and enable me to place the document in his hand?'

'He is a busy man,' Ella returned.

'I expect so.'

'He's a difficult man.'

'That is to be expected.'

'He lived with me in this house a while back.'

'You told me.'

'Ah – yes – I told you. He was an importunate guest. We had too much morality with the Puritans, but now we have too little. Sir Wilson Broadbent has no morals.'

'But I also expect that he owes you a favour.'

'Well – did I not tell you that I detest him and have been avoiding him like the plague?'

'I beg your pardon, Ella, if I embarrass you. Would you prefer me to ask Mr Westington to summon Sir Wilson?'

'No, no – they have fallen out somewhat.'

'I could pretend not to know it.'

'No, Alice, I do not want Sir Wilson's name mentioned in my husband's hearing. You must promise me not to inflame Desmond's feelings. I could not abide a duel and the possibility of bloodshed.'

'Ella, we could meet Sir Wilson accidentally in Hillaby Square. Who would be the wiser? It would take two minutes to transact my business. Do me this good turn and I will give you my solemn promise never to betray you.'

'Oh Alice,' Ella yielded and agreed.

The two young women composed a suitable summons for Sir Wilson, directed a servant to carry it to St James's Palace and waited for his response. A messenger brought it: Sir Wilson would walk in Hillaby Square at four o'clock of the same day. Ella and Alice were seated on a bench at the time in question. He emerged from the shrubbery, bewigged and overdressed in the Carolean style, all bows and buckles. Under his hat and between his curls he had a jowly red face and twinkling eyes, and was aged about forty.

'Mistress Ella—' he exclaimed on seeing her.

She interrupted: 'Pray choose your language more carefully, sir!'

He grimaced with mock terror and inquired: 'Is the lion about who refuses to share his prey?'

'He is safe in his office. Sir Wilson, I have sought your assistance for my friend Mrs Widell, who is fresh from the country and would speak with you.'

Sir Wilson addressed Alice: 'I can see you are as fresh as a daisy, Madam.'

'I could say the same of you,' Alice retorted.

Amidst laughter Ella proceeded: 'Mrs Widell has a favour to ask – and I think you owe me one.'

Sir Wilson smirked and said to Alice: 'What can I do for you, dear lady?'

'You have an important post at Court, Sir Wilson, and I would be infinitely grateful if you would convey a letter from my husband into the hand of His Majesty.'

'Infinite gratitude always excites me, Madam. Is that to be my only task this lovely afternoon?'

'In my eyes no other task accomplished would give me equal gratification.'

'Alas! Oh well – let me look at the lines and read between them.'

'It is private correspondence, sir.'

'And I am King Charles's Private Secretary.'

'The letter is sealed, sir.'

'No matter – I can reseal it – and I could not present any written matter to the King that might displease him.'

Alice, embarrassed for once, with pink in her cheeks and downcast eyes, handed it over.

Sir Wilson asked after perusing the document: 'Is this the signature of your husband?'

'It is.'

'Who wrote the letter in that case? Did you?'

'Yes.'

'Is your husband aware that he endorsed this sentence, "My well-favoured wife will be proud to do your Majesty the honours of the house"?'

'Sir, he is a countryman and does not go in for reading.'

'Well said, Madam. I will do as you wish, and hope the consequences will give pleasure to all concerned.'

Alice thanked him and extended her hand for him to kiss.

'Ladies,' he said, 'my carriage is round the corner and we could adjourn to it and dally there undisturbed.'

Ella declined.

'No, Sir Wilson, I think our books are balanced now. Besides, I am sure I have heard Mr Westington's voice – he must have returned early. Thank you and goodbye.'

'I retire – I do not rush, please note – I retire regretfully, and drat the husbands,' Sir Wilson replied.

The two young women exchanged satisfied smiles and sauntered homewards.

Ella remarked, 'All is explained,' and Alice made a different point: 'Each of us has a secret to keep.'

The Widells' invitation was accepted. King Charles the Second, together with his retinue of court officials, servants, coachmen, grooms and an armed guard, would spend the night at Widell Manor in Gorham in twelve months' time. Hector Widell was alarmed, Alice delighted, the local establishment jealous, the populace astounded. A huge building programme was set in motion, two wings tacked on to the house, stables added, also a new row of cottages for the soldiery, and pleasure grounds with sculptural features.

An advance party of courtiers arrived in the morning of the appointed day. They had complaints and insisted on changes, but by five o'clock, as dusk fell on a September afternoon, everyone and everything was ready for the royal visitor. Heralds with trumpets preceded his coach, his cavalcade was lit by flaming torches, there were cheering crowds, and the dark-visaged man, wearing a luxuriant wig and a hat with a curling feather, showed gratitude and grace as he waved to his subjects and was welcomed by the Mayor and Mrs Smithers and a deputation of notabilities.

His Majesty reached Widell Manor eventually. Hector introduced his wife, whose curtsy in a low-cut gown could well have reinforced the message in her letter, and they escorted their guest to his suite of rooms. After a two-hour period set aside for the King to rest after his journey and to prepare for the evening's festivities, he joined the assembled company in the Widells' new Banqueting Hall. Following speeches of greeting and introductions, he deigned to take his seat at the head of the U-shaped table between Hector on his left and the Mayor, Archibald

Smithers, on his right – Alice sat opposite him on the inner curve of the U.

Then toasts were drunk. Alice was aghast: Hector had disobeyed her order that toasting should not begin until the meal was at an end. She had rubbed it in since Hector had had recourse to Dutch courage earlier in the day. He now tripled his offence, drinking bumpers to His Majesty, his restoration and his health, and stumbling increasingly over his verbiage. Inevitably, as a result, the Mayor followed suit, and in time a dozen more toasts were proposed by persons sitting below the salt. The consequences were catastrophic verging on farcical. The host was stupefied, the serving of food was interrupted, conversation was almost out of the question, and disrespectful and even raucous laughter was heard as one self-important man after another rose unsteadily to his feet.

It was not what Alice intended. However, as her banquet deteriorated into a rowdy party, her relationship with the guest of honour developed largely by ocular means. Across the dinner table their eyes kept on locking in glances, receptive, understanding, patient, resigned, and, on his side, humorous and amused.

She quite fell in love with his dark deep eyes, his eyes which were a bonus over and above his monarchical attractions.

They had one short snatch of dialogue just before it was time for the ladies to leave the gentlemen to discuss serious matters as best they could.

The King leant forwards, she did likewise, and he said to her: 'I have sympathy for your situation, Madam.'

'Oh, Sire, thank you.'

'Loneliness is a condition we are both acquainted with.'

'Oh Sire!'

'Do not trouble yourself, I have fared worse than I fare at present.'

And he smiled at her so charmingly that she was aware of a powerful weakness in her knees.

About an hour later she received word via royal servants that His Majesty was ready to retire – he had had a long day.

Alice waited in the hallway outside the Banqueting Room. The King emerged, arm-in-arm with and supporting Hector Widell. She was mortified – she signalled to her servants to take charge of the tipsy and tearful Squire – and expressed the hope that His Majesty would pardon her husband and permit her to lead him to his chamber.

He bowed affirmatively.

They mounted stairs, and he requested assistance.

'Madam, take my hand if you will, I do not see so clearly by night light.'

She then inquired: 'Is all to your satisfaction in your room, Sire?'

'There is a fault in the mattress, Madam.'

'You horrify me, Sir – what's wrong?'

'No queen lies on it.'

She laughed. They laughed.

He added: 'Could you repair the omission? You gave me a hope and almost a promise in your missive, Mistress Widell.'

'My name is Alice, Sire.'

'You do not answer my question.'

'Sire, I would obey any royal command.'

He then led her by the hand into his bedroom.

Three hours later, in the smallest hours, Alice returned to her own nuptial couch, in which Hector lay comatose.

'Wake up, Sir,' she said. 'Stir yourself! You have one more duty to perform.'

She achieved a response from him sufficient for her to say: 'Thank you, my dear. We must never forget this compliment you have paid me. You will remember it, won't you, Hector? It was a perfect climax to a perfect day, wasn't it? Wasn't it?'

'Damn good,' he panted and went back to sleep.

The King left Gorham in the morning.

Nine months later Alice bore Hector a son, who was christened Theodore Hector Charles. She felt, in respect of the boy's names, that she was distributing thanks diplomatically for his birth.

Hector was proud of little Theodore. He attributed the darkness of the child's visage to his heredity: 'Old Theodore, my great-great-whatever he was, he had a touch of Spanish onion, they used to say.'

One morning at breakfast he laid down his knife and fork and remarked to his wife: 'By jingo, Alice, it's come back to me that you went to see that doctor in London to get yourself broody. You were clever to do it, and he must be cleverer than most quacks. What's his name? I'd like to send him a cask of ale to thank him for our Theodore.'

'He's dead.'

'Dead, is he? Was he ailing when you saw him?'

'Not at all.'

'What did he die of?'

'I've no idea, Hector. I don't like to think of the days before we produced our darling.'

'I wonder if the doctor's widow enjoys a tipple. I'd like to reward somebody, you know.'

'Well, you can reward yourself. You begat one boy. And we're almost back in begetting mood again.'

'Good Lord!'

But Hector was sleepier, and Alice was not ready to shake him into wakefulness as she had for the sake of Theodore. She proposed instead a celebratory visit to London – she wished to show her son to her friend Ella, she said, who had invited the three Widells to Hillaby Square. Hector rejected the offer in accordance with his wife's design. She wrote a letter to Sir Wilson Broadbent, and arrived at the Westingtons' home with Theodore and his nursemaid.

Ella took one look at the boy and called him regal. She presented Alice with an envelope containing Sir Wilson's answer. Both women read it and clucked disapprovingly.

Sir Wilson wrote: 'Madam, thank you for yours. I remember you well. You ask for a brief audience with His Majesty. My role at his Court is similar to the ancient one of King's Taster. I expect and am expected to eat first of all that His Majesty is about to eat, in case the food should be unclean. I trifle, Madam. In truth, I am appointed to please my Master by all available means. I therefore suggest that you call upon me at five-thirty at the above address, when I shall conduct you along the path trod by many pretty feet into His Majesty's presence. I beg to remain yours, etc.'

Punctually on the day in question, Alice Widell was ushered by Sir Wilson Broadbent into the Audience Chamber of St James's Palace, where King Charles sat alone on a throne-like chair.

'My dear lady,' he greeted her, rising to his feet and approaching.

She curtsied, he raised her up, and, after a polite preamble, they spoke their minds.

'Sire, I have borne you a beautiful son.'

'A love-child, dear Alice. What does your lord and master think?'

'He is proud.'

'He is therefore wiser than he seemed to be.'

'He is a worthy man, Sire. He is your loyal subject, as my first husband who fought for your father was, God rest his soul, and I am and shall always be.'

'Have I debts to clear? Should I pay Widell for the upkeep of my child?'

'You are known for your generosity, Sir.'

'Well, you were generous, my pretty Alice, and I would like to be remembered fondly by yourself and your family. I own a farm near your home – it shall be yours and I will create your spouse Baron Gorham of Goatsacre.'

'Sire, it is all I ever hoped for. How can I thank you?'

'Unfortunately, I am enslaved by the clock. Perhaps, another time, you will thank me as I know you can. Now, I have to bid you good evening.'

'Will you not see your son, Sir? He is outside with his nurse.'

'My dear, forgive me, I have seen so many.'

Topsy-Turvy

Alice Widell, with her son and his nurse, returned from St James's Palace to Hillaby Square, and gave Ella Westington the news that she was about to be a ladyship.

Ella's congratulations took a bitter form. She did not look pleased, and said, referring to the baby and the barony: 'You've killed two birds with one stone.'

Alice was hurt in her feelings, but reflected with complacence that the world in general had reason to envy her, and would and could have an extra reason in the near future.

Home and her husband brought her down to earth. Hector's fondness for alcohol was almost exclusive. He had a new excuse for making a slobbery fool of himself: he had been so flattered by the royal choice of his roof to sleep under, by King Charles's condescension, that he had formed a habit of drinking a health to His Majesty. He began at breakfast and continued until he was carried to bed. Alice scolded and he apologised repeatedly, but he continued to raise his elbow.

At last the document drawn up by the College of Heralds was delivered by King's Messenger.

The Widells were breaking their fast one

morning . 'What have we here, dear?' Hector
giggled at the rhyme. 'What's in it, old girl?'

'I am not old, Hector.'

'Sorry – be a sport – read it to me!'

'You're to be a lord.'

'What's that?'

'You're to be Lord Gorham – we're to be Lord
and Lady Gorham – the King has raised us up
– we're the Gorhams of Goatsacre.'

'What's Goatsacre got to do with it?'

'King Charles has given us Goatsacre Farm –
it's very big – we shall be twice as rich.'

'Is it a joke, Alice?'

'Of course not – look at the seals!'

'How could he be so good to me? He must
love me as I love him. God bless His Majesty!
I'll drink his health, by jingo!'

'You've been drinking it since daybreak.'

'What of it? I'd do anything for my King,
and I hope you'd do the same, Alice.'

'Well – not quite the same – and I want to
warn you, Hector – you're not taking your seat
in the House of Lords until you're steady on
your feet. Stop drinking – do you hear me?'

'We've all got to drink, my dear.'

'Not the liquid that makes you even more of
a fool than you are.'

'That's no way to speak to your husband,
specially now he's a lord – your lord as well as
your master.'

'Oh Hector!'

'Pray remember that I am a favourite of my
King.'

'Oh Hector!'

'For the King's sake I shall be sober when I need to be.'

'Oh Hector,' she repeated, making rueful comparisons.

In the days that followed she was annoyed by Hector's assumption that he alone had earned the title, and that she could not set the record straight. Again she was annoyed when her husband did moderate his drinking, because his utterances became understandable and were even more boring than they had been. He also ceased to be impotent, and the next and worst thing was that he finally got her with child.

She disliked her second son from the word go – he did not fit into her scheme of things – she had hoped that Theodore Hector Charles would always be the sole recipient of her love.

She called the boy Walter, not a nice name by her standards. He was an eyesore compared with Theodore, bald and wan whereas his brother had red cheeks and flashing dark eyes and black curly hair. Walter was featureless, glum rather than cheery, and silent long after the other had learned to chatter fluently. She gave him no benefits of the doubt, and declared openly that he was a weed sullying the garden of her world. His shyness was certainly exacerbated by his mother's yielding to the temptation to make him blush and cry.

It was not Theodore's fault that he was such a darling. His mother played with him. She grudged his nurses the time they had him to themselves. She kissed him good night until he slept, and encouraged him to kiss her good morning and climb into bed with her. She let him tell her the shaggy dog stories that children inflict on grown-ups – Walter was never encouraged to make himself heard. She was happier for longer with Theodore than she had been with any other member of the opposite sex.

And she wove fantasies around their future. She imagined that he would be plucked from obscurity and placed upon the throne – the how and the why were unexplained. He would become King Theodore the Good and she would be Queen Mother. She saw him galloping into battle ahead of his army, brandishing the Royal Standard. She had golden dreams in which he laid the spoils of conquest at her feet. She also had a nightmare in which he got married. She tempted fate by thinking that nothing worse than his marriage some time never could happen.

An epidemic announced its presence in Gorham by the tolling of the church bell. A death on one day was followed by two deaths on another, and so it progressed mathematically and without mercy. Dr Pennyfeather was nonplussed. The disease was not always lethal, but when it killed it did so in a matter of hours or even minutes. Hector, Lord Gorham, insisted that it was reserved for the common people, and that nobles and their children were inviolate.

As usual, he was wrong. He contracted the disease, lingered for two days and nights and expired. Alice was shocked, but could not be sorry.

At his funeral, the wickedest prayer occurred to her. She prayed that the second Lord Gorham who sat beside her, holding her hand in his little one, might be spared if fate would make do with Walter, who sat on the other side.

Fate chose Theodore.

She was shattered. She cried outwardly and inwardly for innumerable moons. Then she took stock of the prospects of herself and the family. Walter the weed had survived. She resented his survival, and still hoped to be rid of the little wretch. In that case the title would die with him, become extinct, and everything she had arranged, worked for, played for, prayed and suffered for, would be nullified. She could neither bear it nor allow it to happen. She therefore composed and wrote a letter to King Charles the Second.

'Sire,' it began, 'your most humble, obedient, devoted and loving servant has to inform you of the death of my husband and of Theodore Hector Charles, the loveliest of boys, beloved by all, and a veritable Prince Charming in the tear-stained view of his mother. As a result of these losses, the barony of Gorham is in peril for reasons too complex to be writ here, unless Your Majesty should grant me eligibility for its inheritance. If the title were to be capable of passing through the female line, and if I were to be its proud holder, my expectation is that I would be a widow at the time in question. But

I am a young woman, Sire, and could make a baby for many years to come. I would find a second husband in name without difficulty, and soon be ready for a lover, in order to produce an heir of one sex or another to the title. I beg Your Majesty to confer this favour, yet another favour, upon me, and must add that I am now at liberty to come to London to prove any of the points in my letter that might be of interest to Your Majesty.'

King Charles's reply was handwritten, an honour in itself, yet at once satisfactory and disappointing.

'Dear Lady,' he wrote, 'You shall have your way with me. The other way round not convenient, alas. Affairs of state are less agreeable. Remembrances, C.R.'

Obstinately, Walter left boyhood behind him and grew to be a youth. He was a stripling with a plain face, spiky hair, eyes like marbles and sticking-out teeth. He seemed to have neither bones nor muscles, he bent in all direction, and began to have spots. He was nothing like a lord, but alive.

Alice could scarcely believe it. Every year that Walter survived seemed to have the effect of ageing her by two or three. She would not have murdered him, but was amazed that nature had not done so. It was not exactly that she craved to be Lady Gorham in her own right; it was that she wished Walter not to represent the family and be the recipient of the munificence of His Majesty. She believed she would do better than he could. The danger of which she was increasingly aware was that Walter might take it into his head, or rather his loins, to mate. The question was, would he ever be potent?

His shyness was not grown out of. He made few friends at school. He wandered the countryside, keeping out of Gorham, where he was more likely to be recognised. He often ate in the kitchen while his mother ate in the dining-room or her bedchamber: neither of them could abide those meals poisoned by her interrogations and his silences. From the age of sixteen he frequented taverns in outlying places, in which he would sit alone and not be bothered by anyone or anything.

He especially liked The Goat in Goatsacre for two reasons. There was a dark corner in which to crouch and imagine he was a sort of king in disguise – nobody knew that he owned most of the surrounding land and a major part of the village. Secondly, he liked the barmaid, Griselda.

He did not speak to her, of course. He did not even let her catch him gazing at her. He would order a tankard of ale and some bread and cheese from the tavernkeeper, and she would prepare and bring him the food. He named no one and no one named him. He did not knowingly lust after Griselda, he was attracted by her kindness – it was so kind of her not to badger him with questions.

Griselda was older than he was, perhaps twenty-one when he was seventeen. She was also taller and heavier – she was a big person with a piglike countenance and rosy red cheeks, and had more a bulky than a shapely figure. She was hard-working, always busy in the tavern kitchen, and escaped the attentions of a few of the men by having to hurry to be somewhere else. She had a nice smile and was blessed with the ability to mind her own business.

For six months or so Walter spent time at The Goat once or twice a week. He enjoyed the routine of his visits. But one midday Griselda brought him his victuals in a different way. She approached sheepishly, without her customary briskness, and curtsied before placing his plate on the table.

'What are you doing?' he mumbled, blushing.

'Beg pardon, my lord,' she returned with downcast eyes.

'Please,' he began.

'Please what?' she queried after a pause.

'Don't call me that,' he mumbled.

'Sorry, sir.'

'Oh no – no – don't be sorry – please. It's all right – everything's all right.'

'Thank you, sir.'

She turned away. But he detained her. There were no customers nearby and he could not be overheard.

'Are you Griselda?'

'Some call me Grisel.'

'But you don't grizzle.'

She burst out laughing, and he joined in as shy people do, suddenly and loudly.

'Why did you call me "my lord"?'

'Mister Hopwood told me.'

'Is he in charge here?'

'It's his, see. He told me you're Lord of Gorham.'

'I'd like you to call me Walter.'

'Oh, I couldn't, sir.'

'I'll call you Grisel and you'll call me Walter. I'd be so pleased if you'd try it.'

'Well...'

'Please, Grisel!'

'I'll do my best. Excuse me, sir.'

'Try again.'

'Excuse me, Walter.'

She giggled, they giggled together, and she covered her mouth with her hand and bustled away with her head down.

They talked again on several other occasions. He dared to ask her: 'Are you Miss or Missis?'

'I'm just Grisel,' she replied, which he took to mean she was not married.

On another day she dared to ask: 'Do you live in a big house?'

He answered: 'I get out as quick as I can.'

'Don't you like it?'

'I hate it.'

'That's sad.'

One day he asked where she lived.

'Back there,' she said, pointing at the kitchen.

'Is it your room?'

'I work for Mrs Hopwood too. She lets me sleep in the pantry.'

'Where's your home?'

'Out East Acre way. I left home long ago.'

'Are you happy, Grisel?'

'That's a funny question. I don't rightly know.'

Their conversations were pleasant for both of them.

It was not too difficult for him to inquire after a month or so: 'Do you have time off, Grisel?'

'Half-days sometimes.'

'Will you come for a walk?'

'Walk what for?'

'We could walk in Woody Forest.'

'What do you want with me, Walter? I don't want you getting me in a muddle.'

'I only want to be your friend.'

'Well I never! Well – I'll see.'

She saw and she agreed. They walked about four miles on a spring afternoon. He told her he was no good at anything, did not like his mother, had lost his father and his brother, and wished he was nobody, not a lord, and responsible for nothing. She consoled him even to the extent of holding his cold and bony hand. She promised that she would walk with him again, and in the end he hugged her gratefully.

On a third walk their talk veered in an intimate direction.

He asked: 'Grisel, have you kissed boys?'

'That'd be telling,' she retorted a trifle sharply.

'I've never kissed anybody,' he confessed. 'My mother doesn't kiss me, although she used to kiss my brother.'

'Are you wanting me to kiss you?'

'No. But I don't know how it's done. Do you?'

'Course I do.'

'Because of boys?'

'I don't kiss much, but everyone knows how to.'

'Except me.'

'That's silly, Walter. I don't mind showing you. But you're not to think I'm free with kisses.'

She touched his lips with hers.

'Is that all?' he asked.

'I'm not showing you no more today,' she replied.

Needless to say that the subject, once broached, was reverted to.

One afternoon on a dry sunny bank in the forest, where they had stopped to rest, she capped another stimulating exchange of secrets by giving him lesson two in kissing.

And in the fullness of time, after practice had pretty well perfected their kisses, he made curious mention of copulation.

'No, no,' she exclaimed, 'I'm not teaching you that, Walter, that's for a better girl than me to teach.'

It was food for thought. Walter was now getting on for eighteen, and his mother was nagging him non-stop. She set him tasks such as climbing a tree to dislodge the nest of noisy rooks or riding an obstreperous young horse. He suspected her of having designs on his life, and said so to Grisel, whose chief objection to the notion was that his death would not profit Lady Gorham.

'Oh but it would,' Walter informed her. 'She'd be queen of the castle if I was out of the way. She'd inherit my rights, she'd inherit the lot, if I was gone and hadn't married and left a child, an heir, behind me.'

Grisel nodded, an indication that she did not understand. But the more Walter chewed on his food for thought the more he understood.

He proposed to Grisel.

Her response was monosyllabic.

'Eh?'

'Will you marry me?' he repeated.

She giggled, she blushed, they both blushed, and she said: 'Oh Walter, you're a good boy, you're a nice man, and you're stupid. I can't marry you. You mustn't marry me. What a shame!'

But he had at last hit on a project into which to inject the energy he had accumulated by the years of his drift and inertia. He demolished the arguments that Grisel was able to advance against the match. He was not a snob, he preferred her class to his. He intended to steer clear of public life. The last thing he wanted was a brainy wife. She suited him. He loved her. And she would be his antidote to his mother.

Grisel objected to his idea that she was to be pig in the middle between his poor mother and himself.

'Not poor,' he corrected her. 'Will you meet her? Come and see for yourself! Please do it for me!'

Reluctantly, after more urgings and encouragement, because she felt indebted to Walter as well as sorry for and fond of him, she gave in.

The two of them burst in on Alice one afternoon. She was alone, doing her needlework in the withdrawing room at Widell Manor, according to her custom and as Walter had expected. He had not warned her he was coming, and he dragged Grisel in by the hand.

'Mother, this is the girl I want to marry. She's the barmaid at The Goat in Goatsacre.'

He almost shouted it out to stop himself stammering or losing his nerve.

She fainted or pretended to; but then recovered with a vengeance and harangued them thus, addressing Grisel first: 'You dirty girl! You minx, you trollop! You'll marry my son over my dead body. I'll have you whipped for catching him between those fat legs of yours.' She turned on Walter. 'You too! She's a peasant. You're not to marry so beneath you and disgrace our family. You're not marrying anyone, not until I tell you, so that's that. Go away, you horrible boy, and take your beastly bitch with you!'

Walter cringed and obeyed her. Grisel was purple-faced and crying.

'Now you know what I've been talking about,' he said.

'Yes,' she sobbed.

'Will you marry me?'

'I might, I might now, to spite her.'

Eighteen months later great changes had occurred in the Widell dynasty. Two Lady Gorhams were to be found in the withdrawing room of the Manor, and neither of them Alice. One was Griselda, who wore widow's weeds, and the other was the third holder of the title, a baby in a cradle, Miranda by name.

Alice Gorham, formerly Widell, previously Wilby, was no more. She had suffered an apoplexy following Walter's introduction of his Grisel to her. And his marriage and then the birth of his daughter Miranda, the heiress presumptive to the title, had been the death of her.

She had recovered her speech after her apoplexy, but made no sense. She raved about the female line, and cursed the day that she had swung it for other women to become as noble as she alone was meant to be. She claimed to have lain with King Charles the Second, borne his son, and should be his Queen: a nurse who attended her said that it was a common symptom of the dementia of older ladies. She was confined to her bedchamber after she was ill and received no visitors – she and her daughter-in-law never actually exchanged a single word, for Grisel had not answered back when Alice abused her. Her last reported words were, 'God save the King and to hell with Widells!'

Her death should have been a new beginning for her son, but his relief was so extreme, and his joy so unnatural, that many thought they brought about his end. He and Grisel had been happily married notwithstanding Alice, and Grisel was correspondingly saddened by bereavement. But her sadness was contaminated by guilt.

Unexpectedly, Walter's manhood was not at all shy. In spite of his skinny build, he bore comparison to a newt from the first night of matrimony onwards. When he sickened and died, she accused herself of having knocked the stuffing out of him and depleted his strength. First her mother-in-law and secondly her spouse seemed to have been casualties of acquaintance with herself.

And she was superstitious, which is the countrified synonym of religious. She had not been spared the knowledge of Alice's curses: her servants had become her candid friends. She was having trouble with motherhood, and she attributed some of Miranda's infantile peculiarities not only to the loss of the child's father but also to the intervention of divinity, egged on by Alice. Perhaps God had made Miranda so large and greedy in order to punish her mother: Grisel wondered if she would be eaten alive. Had the Lord of lords given Miranda those dominant features, the potato nose, the bestial mouth, and the ferocious personality, to teach Grisel not to kill people?

No doubt such negative fancies were post-natal as well as inspired by grief and bewilderment. Grisel found a wet-nurse for the baby, and her mourning for Walter was more or less replaced by the need to cope with practicalities. Correspondence bearing columns of figures was delivered to Widell Manor. Her head reeled because the numbers referred to money that was said to be hers. She did not believe it, she could understand nothing, and a gentleman called Bickerstaffe complicated the issues by coming to see her.

He almost forced an entry, strode into her presence without an invitation, alarmed her with his gentlemanly bearing and grey hair, and introduced himself.

'My lady,' he said, 'I am Mr Bickerstaffe of Bickerstaffe, Ames and Higgins.'

He bowed to Grisel and she curtsied to him, which caused him to frown.

'I am a lawyer, my lady,' he said.

'Oh gracious,' she exclaimed fearfully.

'We are the lawyers who have acted for the Widell family for many years, and we will be looking after your financial affairs in future.'

'How kind of you, sir.'

Mr Bickerstaffe cleared his throat.

'It will be a business relationship, my lady.'

'I'm sure you don't need to bother, sir – I wouldn't want to bother you.'

He cleared his throat again.

'My lady, you will be reimbursing my firm for our services.'

'Beg pardon, sir, I didn't catch your meaning?'

'You will be paying us, Madam. We will be serving you.'

'Oh, that won't do, your serving me, sir – it should be the other way.'

'No, Madam. There is only the one way. We work for you and you pay for our work. Now, where is the late Lord Gorham's will?'

'Lord Gorham wasn't ever late, sir.'

'I meant the deceased Lord Gorham, your husband, Madam. Where is his will?'

'Who is this Will, sir?'

'What is it, my lady – what, not who – his lordship should have indicated in writing any or all of his wishes in respect of the disposition of his estate – are you saying that he failed to draw up such a document?'

'Oh sir, I can't answer such questions, though I would like you to know that my Walter never did fail, and there's his child Miranda to prove it.'

'I was not casting aspersions, my lady.'

'Oh sir, you're far above me, I can't make head nor tail of your language. Please tell me common and straight.'

'Thank you, my lady. You are clearly Lord Gorham's sole heir, and I imagine and trust that your instruction will be for us to manage your affairs as we managed his. You will not wish to change anything?'

'No, sir.'

'Very good, my lady. I shall send you a letter and you will countersign the copy.'

'Whatever you say.'

'Please accept my personal condolences, Lady Gorham.'

'Oh no presents, please, sir.'

'I see – no – well – good morning!'

Gradually, Grisel adjusted to Mr Bickerstaffe and their respective roles in society. She could recognise his grey head and remember his name and to call him by it. She even ceased to be startled by visitations from Mr Ames and Mr Higgins. And she had a stock answer to their mysterious questions: 'No change, nothing to be changed, if you please,' which seemed to satisfy or at least to shut her lawyers' traps.

The one change she herself sanctioned and introduced was to shed staff at Widell Manor. When she and Miranda were the only persons on one side of the green baize door, and no guests were invited into the house, she objected to a butler, footmen, odd job men, a cook and scullions, a housekeeper and tweenies on the other side. She did not replace absentees, she encouraged retirement, and raised no objections when notices were handed in. She herself filled the vacant posts. She was pleased to have something to do, something different from struggling to bring up her daughter.

Miranda was never easy, but she began to be more difficult as soon as she could lisp the words 'Shut up ... Silly idiot ... I shall! ... Shove off.'

Miranda was like no forebear. Her father had been shy, her mother was humble, yet she was imperious. Walter had been a bit too like a maypole, Griselda was a bit too like a cottage loaf, but they were not extraordinary, whereas Miranda was years older than her age in size and in mental development, and her face was large and already hairy. Her happy moods were half-mad, her demonstrations of affection knocked people over, her scowls were ominous, and she smashed things when she was upset: characteristics unknown in the annals of the family. They were foreign to Grisel, and she could not cope with them. She had the foresight to dread the future.

At nine years of age Miranda wanted to entertain friends she had made at school. She demanded large teas, and rooms prepared for her friends to sleep in. Grisel was overworked: 'Get more servants,' she was told.

Aged ten, Miranda had breasts and massive buttocks and was pubic. She hunted innocent boys who came to tea and debagged them – she had girlfriends for slaves and accomplices. She shocked her mother. She cowed her mother. The atmosphere at the Manor was tense. Some parents would not allow their children to go there. But no other house in the neighbourhood was so big; no other family so obviously well off despite Grisel's penny-pinching; underage peeresses of the realm did not grow on trees; and Miranda was reckoned by the majority to be a card.

At fourteen she was a rebellious young woman with a gang and a bad reputation for cheeking her elders and betters. Her behaviour, judged by all the prevailing social standards, was bad to an unprecedented degree. Grisel awaited the announcement of an unwanted pregnancy. But the crisis had not been bargained for. Miranda wanted money, not more pocket money, not double her pocket money of a few shillings a week, but twenty pounds or guineas, the equivalent of at least a thousand in the currency of the twenty-first century. Why? She owed it. What? How?

'Betting,' the girl explained in long-suffering accents.

Grisel could not grasp it. She could not believe it. She was not going to pay for gambling. She had no money whatsoever to spare – she and her daughter lived on a monthly pittance from Messrs Bickerstaffe and co.

She asked faintly: 'Bets on what?'

'Races, anything,' Miranda snapped.

'Where did you get the money to bet with?'

'I didn't. I got debts. Don't fuss, Mother!'

But Grisel could not stop. She developed pains in her chest. Then, a day or two after the scene with Miranda, she received a deputation from Messrs Bickerstaffe, Ames and Higgins, all looking grave and judgmental. Young Lady Gorham had marched into their offices and demanded money. Young Lady Gorham had sworn at and threatened them. What were they to do?

Grisel's response was to cry and then to groan and fall to the floor. The strains of marriage above her station and mothering a monster had stretched her constitution beyond its capabilities. She could answer no more awkward questions. She took to her bed and began to fade away. One more conversation with Miranda hastened her end.

She summoned the girl to her bedside and said: 'Unless you mend your ways you're going to blacken our name. Oh I do fear for you! I see you coming to grief!'

'I bet you I won't,' Miranda retorted.

*   *   *

Fifteen years later the forecast of Griselda Lady Gorham seemed to be coming or to have come to pass.

Miranda had grown into a gross shapeless woman nearing the age of thirty. Her inheritance had not been huge, since the lawyers had mismanaged it on her mother's instructions or lack of them, but she had already run through more than half of it. She had married a man who called himself Plantagenet and claimed to be descended from King Richard the Second. She gave birth twice, but her two sons were stillborn. Richard Plantagenet was a professional gambler, but unprofessional as he lost money steadily, her money. He was debonair and feckless. He turned out to be a criminal on the run, real name Richard Clark, and when he felt in danger of being apprehended by the law he took ship to America without bidding his wife goodbye. He died in a saloon bar brawl, according to information she received together with a note in her husband's hand, which ran: 'To my widow. Odds are I will be in hell when you read this. Raise a glass to the memory of me, my lady! Best of luck when you rattle those dice.'

Miranda had never thought of disclaiming her title and calling herself Plantagenet. She said that by bagging the surname of kings she would have felt a fraud as well as a fool: she had guessed belatedly that her first marriage was bigamous. She did not remarry. She had every reason to suspect that the men in her circle who proposed to her were no better than Richard

Clark; and the remains of her resources could not support another fortune hunter.

Widell Manor under her guardianship was a rowdy and some said a bawdy house. It was a sort of oasis, a drinking hole, free for all, provided you played the game or games in progress. In other words, you could get drunk there, but were likely to lose your money since quite a few of the other guests were sharp and crooked. The party had lasted for a decade and a half. There were cards as well as dice on offer, and bets were also placed on races by horses, flies on windows, mice and snails. Only people who were not respectable entered via the open door, unmarried men, rebellious men, and girls with brains in the wrong place, and poor older women. They often slept there, alone or together, in bedrooms or on the floor, and woke more or less ready for further revels. The fabric of the Tudor-style building shook with laughter – or was it with sobs?

Miranda presided. She was strong enough to keep going physically. She throve on risk and excitement, and seemed to have a masochistic streak considering her history of losses. She laughed loudest and created a jovial atmosphere until her mood changed, she attacked a guest verbally or with her fists, and occasionally chased everyone out of the house for a couple of hours. She was too busy with her gambling, rows with lawyers, disposal of property, and her hospitality and houseful of punters, to enter into personal relations. She was a bizarre force of nature, and seemed to compensate for her size and ugliness by attempting to get the better of luck which had dealt her a preponderance of bad cards.

One stormy night Widell Manor was fuller than usual. Men drifted in to get out of the weather. Musicians were summoned, dancing ensued. Wine circulated and the night turned into morning. Footmen replaced candles yet again, and tried to keep track of the candles in the rooms on the upper floors. One of them raised the alarm. A small fire had been started by a candle in a candlestick knocked over by a tipsy guest who had gone into an empty spare room to sleep. The footman smelt the smoke, entered the room, rescued the sleeper, and fetched water to extinguish the flames, by which time the fire had spread. He hurried downstairs, took more time to find the butler, who hurried up to inspect the damage. Still more time elapsed while the assembled company, musicians, staff and pets were pushed and pulled out of front and back doors; and the house burned down.

Miranda gambled on how long it would take to be ashes. She roared with laughter and slapped her bulging thighs. She said it was a pretty sight. She said, 'Who cares? I don't!' A couple who had often been her guests offered her shelter in their home. She stayed with them for a week: much to their relief, she then moved into The Goat in Goatsacre.

The old host of The Goat, Mr Hopwood, had died and his son John was now in charge. He was forty years old, large and jolly, like his father but shrewder and tougher. He knew Lady Gorham personally and by repute, and was ready to let her have his two residential rooms, payment for them to be weekly in advance. Miranda quibbled; he advised her to go elsewhere; she caved in, instructed Messrs Ames and Higgins – Mr Bickerstaffe had passed over – to find the money. Once installed, she ordered food and drink and invited some of her cronies to come and share it with her. John again wanted cash in his hand for all the extras. She swore and put it there, and tried to run card games in the bar room: he was not having that, and again he prevailed.

Miranda said to herself and others that The Goat was temporary accommodation; but she knew she had nowhere else, nowhere familiar, no practical place of her own, to live in comfortably. Moreover, she was attached to the tavern not merely because her mother had once been its barmaid, but because a tiny spark flashed and crackled between herself and its landlord. John had been the downfall of women. He had pinned up a letter in the bar addressed thus: 'For The Goat, at The Goat, in Goatsacre' – it was from a discarded conquest. But he was still single. He differed from the run of men Miranda had known in that he got the better of her. She swallowed her pride and arrogance, and stayed put. She was tending as best she could the spark that might become a fire to care about.

The state of her finances was no longer possible to ignore. Ames and Higgins – she showed her feelings for them by dropping their Misters – brought her bad news along with money to pay her bills. They had sold on her behalf the Forest of Woody, the village of Wood Houses, the land adjacent acquired by her forefather Theodore, her cottages in Gorham, and so on and so forth. Since the destruction of Widell Manor, her credit-rating had slumped – shopkeepers required payment on the nail. The lawyers' own fees were outstanding, and mounting up. Her only hope, they said, was to sell the last metaphorical jewel in her crown, the Goatsacre farmhouse and farm: it would raise enough money to clear her debts, rebuild a dwelling on the site of Widell Manor, and give her a sufficiency to support her for the remainder of her life.

'No,' she shouted at them, 'no, no!'

She hated them. She detested defeatism. She refused to discuss her remaining days. She was still determined not to admit her mother had won the bet that she would be the ruin of herself and her family. She confided in John, although it might be unwise to warn him that she was near bankruptcy. He had another reputation, for being astute with money. He was said to be a gambler in a quiet way, not in her category, not the sort she knew, but one who actually made a profit.

He agreed to think over her predicament. For weeks, then months, she asked him if he had finished thinking. He smiled and shook his head. Her predicament grew worse.

At last he invited her into his private room

behind the bar. She was interested to accept for more reasons than one. They sat on either side of a table covered with a flowered cloth.

'I've three thoughts to lay before you, my lady,' he said. 'First thought is you could follow the advice of the lawyers and sell up everywhere.'

'What's second?' she inquired.

'You could marry me.'

She laughed, burst out in a sweat, did not know where to look, banged her fist on the flowered table cloth without knowing why.

He continued: 'It's insolence, I know. It'd be a step down for you and a step up for me. But I'm richer than you are at present. I knew your ma when she worked for my pa, so we've got our connections already. We're neither of us young, and we could be content together. I've a fancy to have a lady wife, and I'm ready to play gentleman. What say, Madam?'

'Can't. You've taken my breath away.'

'Sorry about that.'

'I'm not saying no.'

'Am I hearing straight?'

'Probably. What's third?'

'Third depends on second, see? I'm richer than you are, but couldn't offer you haven and home at The Goat. Suppose it was to be yes, I wouldn't want you to lower yourself, and I wouldn't want a real Lady to be landlady of this old place.'

'Not important,' she mumbled.

'Oh but it is. It is to me, and I'd be having the say-so. There's a chance to make more money than The Goat's worth. I'm halfway to cashing in the tavern and buying shares in a company I know of. Supposing I should be lucky, I could build somewhere private and do farming in a small way. It wouldn't be Widell Manor that was, I'd be ashamed to carry you over the threshold, if I could carry you, but it would be better than you and me serving beer.'

They both laughed.

She now found her voice and asked with a glitter in her eye: 'What's this company?'

'Deals in goats and things on the other side of the world.'

'Goats are a coincidence. What are the odds, John?'

'Steady now – I'm a cautious man – don't you run ahead of me, my lady!'

'Please say?'

'Two to one anyway.'

'Sure?'

'Sure as can be. I never will say more. But I've done well with chances.'

'What if I were to sell Goatsacre Farm and buy shares too?'

'That'd be going it.'

'That's how I always go. What if, John?'

'Likely we'd have enough to build on a bigger scale. But I don't take nothing for granted. My reckoning is that money wouldn't be lost, and a big gain's going begging.'

'Let's do it.'

'Say that again, please.'

She blushed and hung her head and stammered:

'Sorry – I meant, let's put our eggs in the same basket.'

He laughed, said 'Done,' and they each shook a large damp hand.

It was called The South Sea Company. John and Miranda's pooled resources amounted to three thousand pounds. They invested it all in shares in the Company. When the Company promised to pay interest even up to one hundred percent, they borrowed another three thousand at a rate of interest high enough to make blood run cold. But the price of the first lot of shares they had bought went up, and the second lot, bought with the other three thousand, followed suit. They were making money in a day sufficient to repay their borrowings and the interest. What had begun in the month of February as an investment, became a speculation, then a magic carpet. Their excitement tracked the price of the shares, that is it kept on rising, as did their interest in each other. Their destinies were entangled in spun gold, and they decided to make it legal in church. They fixed the date for August and sold all their shares in July. Their six thousand pounds had turned into sixty thousand, give or take a few thousands, and at that date, the early seventeen hundreds, compared with nowadays, they were rich beyond their estimates or their dreams.

Both Sides of the Medal

Three days after Lady Gorham of Goatsacre married John Hopgood in St Mary's Church in Gorham the South Sea Bubble burst. The shares they had held were again worth no more than they had paid for them; if they had still been shareholders, their three thousand pounds of combined capital would have belonged to the usurer who lent them the other three thousand. One consequence was that Miranda was cured of gambling. She had won her bet with her mother, had had more luck in the end than she deserved or anyone could ask for, and she set about reforming her character.

She and John were made for each other. Miranda was soon pregnant and gave birth to a healthy boy. He was called Ernest in hopes that he would be less prodigal than his mother had been. He was further proof of the unpredictability of the process of human reproduction: although both his parents were outsize, he was no bigger than normal and light-boned.

The family bought a modest house in open country between Gorham and Goatsacre, and lived there while they began to build their future permanent home. It was to be grand, beautiful, in parkland, and filled with treasures. Gorhambury would be its name, nothing more than the one word – but the 'bury' derived from borough and meant that it would be superior to a house, grange, manor, court or towers, yet might not qualify as a palace.

They bought back Goatsacre Farm, the Forest of Woody, Wood Houses now known as Woodhouses or Woodhouse, the old Widell lands, and the site of Widell Manor where they intended to build fifty new cottages. Because they had money to play with, and John was honest, neighbouring landowners in difficulties offered him property, and thus the Gorhambury Estate was created.

Miranda had no other children. She subsided into a wife and mother – or perhaps a mother and wife in that order. She doted on little Ernest, and on Ernest as boy and as youth, and let John expend his energies on turning one fortune in cash into a much larger inheritance for their son in articles of solid worth, fields, woods, bricks and mortar, works of art, not to mention rents.

The Lady and her mister lived into the middle of the eighteenth century. They were interred in the graveyard of the chapel attached to Gorhambury and recently roofed and consecrated. Their remains in lead coffins were placed in the luxurious family tomb which occupied most of the space in the graveyard: they slotted into shelves in the underground chamber.

Ernest Theodore, fourth holder of the barony,

was in truth a nobody. He was normal to the point of making not much impression on anyone. On the other hand, he was well aware of his position and power, and proved it by means of his pomposity. He was fair-haired and affected an overlong moustache parted in the middle.

His matrimonial history showed how far the status of the family had changed. Local contenders for the privilege of looking after him in sickness and in health were never in the running. Only a female distinguished by birth and by dowry would deserve a slice of his plutocratic cake. Applicants, or their mothers, existed. Ernest was invited to balls in London by hostesses he did not know, where debutantes sought the 'scope' that his wedding ring on a finger would guarantee. He also stayed in the family seats of rural magnates with an excess of daughters. At last he surrendered to Lady Candida Mallochstrane, a hard-faced and humourless Scottish Presbyterian who was due to inherit fifty thousand acres of barren hillsides.

Ernest and his Candida – his in name, he was hers in effect – were dutiful. They somehow produced an heir, Hamish Theodore. They lived in the finished wing of Gorhambury, and spent a large proportion of their income on building and increasing the size of the stately rooms planned by his parents. Candida decided that the word 'Goatsacre' was improper, it sounded like 'goat sucker' and might have originated as such, and neither herself nor her husband should be associated with it. They devoted their energies for many years to getting the s deleted, and were eventually pleased to be Lord and Lady Gorham of Goatacre.

In the fullness of time Hamish Theodore succeeded to the title. He was a throwback to his grandparents, Miranda and John Hopwood, being large and loud; and he inherited the single-mindedness or narrow-mindedness of Ernest and Candida. He was the first Widell to know he was rich enough to be idle and to please himself. His instinct was to kill things: he said he considered a day wasted on which he had not killed a fellow creature. He hunted foxes, deer, hares, badgers and otters. He formed the Gorhambury Hunt and employed an architect to build kennels for his hounds. He shot in Scotland in the autumn, shot pheasants, partridges, snipe and woodcock when he was not hunting throughout the English winter, destroyed vermin in the summer months, and again devoted himself to sport on his Scottish property. He married a girl who was pretty and poor, he could afford her, and they had issue, the presumptive Archibald in particular.

Archie was another nonentity – he betrayed it by his self-importance. His appearance was Scottish, red-haired and red-faced, and he became fixated on his connections with Scotland. He wore a tam o'shanter in the Home Counties and sported a ghillie's walking stick, elongated and horn-handled, in the environs of the Houses of Parliament. His evening dress was kilt with sporran, dirk, buckled shoes, velvet jacket and lace jabot. He claimed to be the Hereditary

Chieftain of the Clan Mallochstrane, and organised a gathering of all the Mallochstranes in the world at his hunting lodge before the grouse shooting began again in August. It was a memorable occasion – anyway not forgotten by the dozen or so persons who turned up. A Canadian Mallochstrane asserted that he was Chieftain, that Archie was an impostor, and a bout of fisticuffs occurred, ending with the host's undignified retreat – he took refuge in his game larder and his guests did not let him out until they had eaten his haggises and drunk the last dram of his whisky.

Archie in his thirties married a sensible widow, May by name, who reined in his Scottish mania and bore him one child, a son and heir, George known as Geordie. They were a happy family until Archie and May departed this life in quick succession in their forties.

Geordie differed from most of his forebears, he was a responsible young man of means, a fair employer, a precocious philanthropist, no fool, and apparently suited to the new optimistic century, the nineteenth. He married young. He was only twenty-one, although already Lord Gorham of Goatacre, and his wife was a teenage sprite. They were a good-looking couple, he handsome with a fine open regard, she deliciously girlish, pretty and playful. She was called Bella, short for Arabella, and the name was not far wrong. Unfortunately she was short of stature and all her measurements were small.

It had been a love match. They romped

101

through the marble halls and state apartments of their marital home, and their peals of laughter disarmed even the older critical members of their household. As is supposed to happen by spoil-sports, soon the laughing ended in tears – but the tears were not exactly sad. She was sick in the mornings and not much better in the afternoons. The cause was suspected, and the best doctor in Gorham was called in despite his ominous surname, Dr Sawyer. Bella was pregnant.

Her pregnancy was like a disease. She was ill, then iller, and so it went on. Dr Sawyer, professional, kindly, flattered to be attending her ladyship in her four-poster bed in a bedroom half as big as his house, repeated that there was no cause for alarm.

But he informed Lord Gorham in a graver tone of voice that his wife was carrying twins.

Geordie Gorham's concern at that stage was not reserved for his wife. Despite his youth he foresaw complications of a non-medical description, and prayed in order of his preferences that the twins would be a boy and a girl, a boy without a survivor, a girl likewise, or no survivors. Two living boys would be the worst news from at least four points of view, testamentary, hereditary, legal and psychological.

Dr Sawyer assembled an expert team for the lying-in. Mr Tighe specialised in pain, Nurse Welling was the midwife and had a girl called Hester in tow, and Nanny Wishthorp and her

102

nursery maid Annie were waiting in the wings. A surgeon, Mr Peal, also stood by; but surgery presented other problems and would only be resorted to in emergency.

Labour began on time. But it lasted for a day, then a night, then another day, and Bella, weakened by nine months of debilitation, was near to death. Everybody was exhausted and increasingly alarmed. In a valiant ultimate struggle, the babies were born but their mother breathed her last. They were boys.

Tears flowed. Regrets and sorrow were general. Dr Sawyer was so stricken that Nurse Welling and Hester had to attend to him. The twins were possibly identical, but Dr Sawyer's ruling as to which was which was confirmed by Mr Tighe and Nurse Welling. At length Geordie was able to name his first-born James and his second son John.

For the widower, the next years were mournful. He missed Bella, and could not look at another woman. And his feelings for his sons were mixed: in his heart he wished they had been sacrificed to save the life of his wife. But he was too reasonable to blame their innocence, and he tried to treat them well and without favouritism. He had to remake his will. He left his younger son a small fortune: John would be rich by accepted standards. In accordance with the custom and rule of primogeniture he had to leave Gorhambury and its estate to the elder, and sufficient money, most of his money, to keep the property in apple-pie order.

His will nonetheless had a damaging effect on his relationship with the boys. He could not feel at ease with John. He was afraid that John would be angry with him if he knew that he had missed a barony and great possessions by a matter of minutes. He had done his best for John, but understood that John might argue that best was not good in the circumstances. He believed and was told that he was powerless to divide the spoils equally – Gorhambury was indivisible, primogeniture made sense and was not to be tinkered with – but he could not meet John's eye, he sought to placate John by spoiling him, then he was cross with John for getting above himself and out of control, and so the vicious circle was almost complete.

What completed it was his relationship with James. With James, who would one day be as well off as he himself was, he suffered from none of the inhibitions caused by John. They were equals in the making. They were comrades in the arms of their lawyers, accountants, bankers and agents. At the same time, Geordie did not want John to see that he had no aversion to meeting the eyes of James. He had to be cross with James sometimes in order not to provoke jealousy in John. Then he found it difficult to be looked at in an uncomprehending and reproachful way by James.

That his elder son was more loveable than his younger one, and that he loved the elder more, were indigestible facts. He could not consciously swallow them, he prayed not to have to do so, but God did not hear his prayers. God in His wisdom aggravated the situation. James grew taller and stronger than his brother. John seemed almost to shrivel, perhaps because he sensed that he came second in everybody's estimation and had drawn the short straw in the materialistic sense.

Finally, eight years after the death of Bella, Geordie met and married a second wife. She was called Helen, and lived up to the name with her renowned beauty and charm. She expected homage and usually got it. She suited Gorhambury, was another treasure to keep in the house, and she allowed that it would be a worthy setting for the jewel that she was.

But she immediately took to James and vice versa; whereupon John took against her, and under pressure from his father argued that he was sure Helen was not a patch on Bella. John developed a morbid fixation to his dead mother, and, knowingly or not, upset his stepmother. Helen found fault with him, called him a pest and a brat to his face, and dragged her husband into the fray in her defence.

Geordie therefore, unwillingly, tackled John. He invited the boy to join him for a walk in the park. John made a sulky excuse. Since Geordie would also have liked to excuse himself, he was irritated by his son and rebuked instead of reasoning with him.

He said: 'Please don't be unco-operative! I've a bone to pick with you.'

They set off together.

Geordie then had to say: 'Sorry I spoke sharply. Anyway, now we can have a chat. I have asked you to be nice to Helen, but she thinks, and I do agree with her, that you're being rather nasty. What about trying again?'

'She's not my mother. She's nothing to do with me,' John replied.

'Yes, she is, she's my wife, and you owe it to me to respect her at any rate.'

'My mother was kind, everybody tells me she was, and she would have loved me, she would have loved me as much as she loved James. Helen doesn't.'

'Doesn't what?'

'She hates me. Now I just hate her back.'

'Those are awful things to say, and not true.'

'You all hate me.'

'What do you mean? You couldn't be more wrong. It's because you think along those lines that you create difficulties for the people who are trying to show they love you.'

'My mother wouldn't have said I was difficult.'

'That's enough, John! You don't know what you're talking about. Your mother wasn't a saint. She wasn't so pretty as Helen, and no better. I'll thank you to keep a civil tongue in your head in future. If I hear of any more bad manners, or see any, you'll be in trouble.'

At this point John ran away from Geordie, who did not pursue him, and was left biting his lip and wishing he had kept it buttoned. He was at once deeply ashamed of having cast aspersions on his beloved Bella and infuriated

106

with John for provoking him to do so. Moreover his anger engulfed both his wives, Bella for dying and becoming John's evil genius, and Helen for not suffering John in silence. In the final reckoning his achievement was to have made himself feel guilty on three counts instead of one, because he had traduced Bella and quarrelled inwardly with Helen, as well as compounding his offences against his younger son.

Several years passed. Helen produced two children. They were girls, Sybil and Sophia, and her potential rivals. She ignored them as much as she could, and left their upbringing to a nanny and their father. When her stepsons came home for the holidays, she was inclined to escape with or preferably without her husband to their new house in London.

Geordie, James and John, and Sybil and Sophia missing their mother, created a stormy atmosphere at Gorhambury. Mallochstrane came in useful: sometimes James sought refuge on the Scottish property, at other times John was sent there on account of his misdemeanours. Geordie thanked God for boarding schools, and hoped that before too long he would be free of fifty per cent of the tribulations of parenthood – the boys would grow up and be elsewhere, working, perhaps married.

But towards the end of a summer holiday, John, aged fifteen and a half, asked his father to come out for a walk: he seemed to wish to turn tables and Geordie agreed apprehensively.

They emerged from the house on to the terrace

with its fine views of the lake and the landscaped hillocks planted with ornamental trees.

'What is it, John?'

'It's bad, Father.'

'It's none of your nonsense, is it?'

'Why do you have to say that? No, it isn't, so I'll tell you straight out – I've been talking to Nurse Welling.'

'Who's she?'

'She was the midwife when I was born.'

'What? How did you get hold of her? Why did you?'

'Can't you guess?'

'Don't play games, John.'

'She says I was born first.'

It was worse than John had warned that it would be. He had contacted not only Mrs Welling, now retired from her midwifery, but also her assistant at Bella Gorham's lying-in, Hester, who had married an officer of the law since then, Bailiff Robinson, and was the mother of three. Hester Robinson had signed an affidavit to say that she believed the twin later called John had been delivered before the twin later called James.

Geordie was in a rage. John had behaved underhandedly, in an ignoble manner, and was threatening possibly to blackmail his father and brother. The future of the whole family was overcast by mischief and by administrative and legal horrors. But how was the information to be dismissed? How could Geordie refuse to consider the righting of an allegedly terrible wrong?

He ground his teeth and said he would have to look into the matter, and John went back to school.

Geordie spoke to Helen, who said she was on James's side and John with his mean little schemes should be told to stew in his own juice.

Geordie resisted temptation and summoned Dr Sawyer, an old man by this time, and asked him to sign another affidavit reinforcing his original confirmation that James was the elder of the twins.

Dr Sawyer dithered. It was many years ago, he said, and his memory was not so good as it had been. Her ladyship's labour had lasted for hours, thirty-six hours, as he remembered, and naturally the team in attendance was exhausted.

He said: 'We were worn out, indeed we were, when we had to decide which twin was which, and, besides, we were so disappointed and saddened to have lost the poor dear lady.' He added that mistakes had been known to occur. He had the greatest respect for Nurse Welling, Mrs Welling in her private life, and confidence in her integrity; but he could not recall Hester. He still believed his choice was correct. Could he have a little time to cudgel his brain before giving his final answer?

Geordie called on Nanny Wishthorp. She had looked after the twins, also Sybil and Sophia for a year or two, had retired and occupied a cottage on the Gorhambury estate. She was embarrassed to find his lordship on her doorstep, she had never seen much of him while she was in service. She was all apologies for her unpreparedness, but invited him in, offered him tea and cake, thanked him effusively for his benevolence, and waited for him to speak.

'Can I count on you to keep a secret, Nanny?'

'That you can, milord.'

'My son John is claiming that he was the first twin to be born.'

'Fancy!'

'If he could prove he was right, he would be the next Lord Gorham and my main heir, and James would be disinherited to a considerable extent.'

'It would never do, milord.'

'I'd like to agree with you. I dread the effect such a change of fortune would have on James, also the legal turmoil. But I need to gather evidence and prove that the original choice was either right or wrong.'

'There wasn't no mistake, milord. James is a lovely boy, always was, he deserves to be a lord. I never could be fond of John, truth to tell and begging your lordship's pardon.'

'Personal feelings shouldn't enter into the decision that has to be taken again. You may remember that I was with my wife when Doctor Sawyer and the others, yourself included, were washing the babies and cleaning up. I am not in a position to express a view. This second decision will have to be taken by the people who were on the spot and present during the birth.'

'What does Doctor say?'

'He's trying to remember. John has apparently spoken to Nurse Welling, and she claims that John was born before James, and her assistant, Hester Robinson, has written an affidavit that makes the same claim.'

'Nurse Welling may have brought a lot of babies into the world, but she's brought a load of wickedness along with them. She has, milord! And Hester, she's Molly Welling's niece, she'd say what she was told to say by Molly. They're greedy people – I know I shouldn't point the finger, but must say for the sake of James that Molly's greedy.'

'Are you talking of bribery and corruption, Nanny?'

'No, milord. All I'm talking about is that James was first into this world. I saw it with my own two eyes, and that's truer than the sayings of some I could mention but won't.'

'Your nursery maid, Nanny – what was she called?'

'Anne, milord, Anne Cleaver, and still working for you. She's in my place in the nursery and keeping an eye on your daughters, though they've got their governess these days.'

'I'm afraid I didn't know, Nanny – there are so many in my house, working away. I'll have a word with Anne when I go home.'

'You could, milord. But Anne wouldn't ever say different from me. She saw what I saw, and she'd wish James well and that he'd be the lord. We'd both swear on the Holy Bible for James.'

'Thank you, Nanny.'

Geordie was slightly relieved, and more so after his word with Anne. But he realised that Nanny might give counterproductive evidence in a witness box; and, secondly, that he had achieved nothing but a sort of draw, two for James, two for John.

His next move was to try to contact Mr Tighe, the so-called pain expert, who had not earned his fee by being on hand to ease the sufferings of Bella Gorham. Geordie had been critical of Mr Tighe during the excruciating hours, had accused him of quackery; he was therefore not altogether sorry to find out the man was dead – he might have stirred the pot by way of revenge.

The opinion of Dr Sawyer was the casting vote in the matter of the Gorham inheritance, and at long last, after his several refusals to be rushed, he supplied it in writing.

'To the best of my knowledge,' he began, 'following three months of serious consideration, I can stand by my warrant that the Honourable James Widell was born before his twin, the Honourable John. Admittedly, my confidence was shaken by the different view taken by Mrs Welling, who could be right, but my final thoughts are that she is not. My mind was also confused by conversations with Mrs Wishthorp, formerly Nanny to the four Widell children, who witnessed the delivery, and agrees with my original choice, but could be wrong; however, again, my final thoughts are that she and I are not. I believe the Hon. James to be the elder son and heir of the present Lord Gorham, yet must beg his lordship and especially the Hon. John to bear in mind and be ready to forgive in their hearts the unavoidable possibility of human error in good faith.'

It was weak stuff, but could have been even less convincing. Geordie hoped that it would enable him to explain to John in private that a majority of witnesses had outvoted Nurse Welling and Hester Robinson, therefore the status quo would remain in force. But Helen informed him that Nanny Wishthorp's tongue had wagged and her daughters wanted to know what was going on. As a result he felt obliged to summon his four children to a meeting, at which he gave a full account of the business and ruled that he wished to hear no more of it, not a word, ever again.

His wishes were disregarded. Sybil took sides with James and Sophia with John, and they began to squabble. On Christmas Eve James and John had a terrible fight, which ended with James losing a front tooth and John's right arm being broken. There was strife below stairs, too – an uncivil war raged throughout the house. And January ushered in a new year and a new and nastier crisis for all the Widells.

Geordie's solicitors, Higgins, Lovelock and Shew – Ames had retired – requested an urgent meeting with his lordship, and, at Gorhambury, showed him a letter from Minley and Joshua, the second law firm in Gorham. The letter from Mr Minley stated that his firm would now be acting on behalf of the Honourable John Widell in the matter of his inheritance.

The formal consequences in the short term – that is, short by the legal clock, lasting for a couple of years – were unsuccessful attempts to clarify in court after court the right of a minor to sue his father, and a multiplication of fees.

The personal consequences could be compared to a slippery slope. A bad situation became worse, and the gloomiest predictions were quickly made to look optimistic. Causes and characters were tempered in the heat of conflict, and an objective observer would have seen no prospect of armistice or peace.

Geordie was cut to the quick by John's recourse to law and to some extent paralysed by it. He had tried reasoning and rage, and did not know what to do next. He handed Mr Minley's letter to John without comment. When John handed it back with a shrug of his shoulders and a bitter smile, he felt like crying.

Geordie could sympathise with his second son; but to split his estate fifty-fifty was out of the question. How could Gorhambury be divided? How could farms, fields, cottages? How could an equitable accommodation be reached with John, who was dead-set on getting the whole inheritance? Moreover, Geordie refused to contemplate remedying one injustice by imposing another on James. Despite the parable of the prodigal son, he drew the line at rewarding the envy and avarice of John by punishing James for his amiability and virtue. He now had reason to admit that John was altogether undeserving. He was tempted to give him nothing, to cut him out of his will – he was definitely not going to collude in a theft or be associated with the creation of a Bad Lord Gorham.

James took after his father. He was hurt by his brother's attitude – his lost tooth was a mere footnote to the story – and by Sophia for siding against him and with John. His way of dealing with all the problems was to stay in Scotland throughout his holidays and to discuss nothing with anyone – at school he and John were in different scholastic streams and did not mingle socially.

The twins reached the age of eighteen, and the fact that James was all that John was not – handsome, clever, sporting, popular – exacerbated all the problems. John seemed to have grown downwards, was stunted, and had large unblinking green eyes and a greenish complexion. He did not leave Gorhambury, he stayed put, he even stayed indoors, as if to protect the property that he hoped would one day be his. He was not good company and impervious to reproaches. Any reference to the trouble he had stirred up would be greeted by a cruel compression of his lips or a savage response.

The crisis was almost criminal. Geordie was notified that a court case was in the offing and that John had two more witnesses to support his claim, a former housemaid called Ida and a former scullery maid called Queenie. In other words, he had a majority on his side by one witness: the servant girls, as they were at the time of the twins' birth, had sworn that they were waiting in a passage while her ladyship screamed and groaned, and they saw the first baby carried into an anteroom through a slightly open door and recognised John.

Geordie accepted the contention of Mr Higgins that John might not be playing fair, and gave his lawyer permission to seek additional information. Ida, now married and a mother of four, disclosed at once that she had been promised a thousand pounds by the young gentleman, to be paid as soon as he had obtained his money. Yes, she had fibbed, but he had assured her it would not be wrong to help him obtain what was rightfully his. She said that Queenie had been offered the same inducement to sign the paper where she was told to. Hester Robinson was a harder nut to crack, but her husband, the Bailiff, said that she had put her name to the affidavit against his will and because she had succumbed to the temptation of a potential bribe. He also volunteered information that Hester's aunt, Nurse Welling, had done her bit for money.

Geordie ordered Higgins to call John's bluff. He then spoke to both twins. He said the past was past, and he had decided to give his younger son without delay the property he had intended to bequeath to him. The property was Goatacre

Farm, its extensive acreage, its numerous cottages and barns, together with part of the Forest of Woody, altogether a fine estate, if not the size of the eventual inheritance of James, but fraught with fewer responsibilities. As the tenant of Goatacre Farm had been rehoused, he wished John to leave Gorhambury immediately and occupy his new home.

John stared at his father, and submitted without thanks or apologies. James, probably dreading trouble still in store, also left Gorhambury – he went to live at Mallochstrane. Geordie suffered further losses inasmuch as Helen decided she was sick of the behaviour of her step-children, even of James who had deprived her of his company, and was moving to London with her daughters, where they would find better husbands than yokels and tally-hos.

Geordie lived alone at Gorhambury, and was robbed of his treasures by John, who would enter the house and walk off with a picture or pieces of silver. Geordie turned a blind eye to it. His conscience was eased by being the victim instead of imagining that he was victimising his son. He became religious. He was a modest man, and happy to find in his God someone who was grander than he was.

James in Scotland married a girl called Flora. They were respectively twenty and seventeen. Meanwhile John was living a racy life at Goatacre with disreputable cronies. In his twenty-first year he quarrelled with one of them, was badly hurt in a fight, no doctor was summoned because everybody was drunk, and he died: apparently the quarrel began because he was accused of doing the dirty with another man's wife. The twins were as unalike in character as in their adult looks. Yet the day after John's death, James in his youth and strength suffered an inexplicable seizure and followed suit.

John left no will, so his property all reverted to his father and the Widell family, and in due course James's widow Flora bore his posthumous child, Theodore.

The Apogee

The new Theodore, the first nineteenth-century Theodore in his cradle, was exceptional. The doctor who delivered him, Dr Macphie, the midwife, Janet Macnicol, his nanny, Nanny Tilyard, the staff of Mallochstrane, and sundry visitors, all thought he was a fine little gentleman; and these people were Scottish and sparing of praise. He had a touch of grace, his glance was perceptive, his smile beneficent, and he evinced vitality and intelligence.

His mother Flora had lost her husband after mere months of marriage and was still only in her eighteenth year. But she was a clever girl, and had realised on her honeymoon that James was depressingly linked with and dependent on the fate of John, who was going to the dogs and would drag others after him. She later acknowledged that the death of her brother-in-law was her own merciful release, and that, although she was sad about James, the tonic of knowing she would not have to spend the rest of her life with two men or at least with one and a half had probably done her baby a power of good.

History had made her apprehensive as the

birth drew near: she was aware that her late mother-in-law had died in childbirth, after bearing the brothers who had fought themselves into premature graves.

Her labour was not hard, as it happened, and lasted no more than three hours; yet when Dr Macphie said to her, 'You have a healthy boy, Mrs Widell,' she replied with sobs, 'You're telling me lies.'

She had feared that the son of James might look and be like John. She took time to convince herself that he had the correct amount of limbs, fingers and toes, and smiled at her sincerely. She christened him Theodore because God had given him to her entire and wonderful after all, as well as to carry on a family tradition.

Although she loved him very much, she was pretty and lonely, and conscious of his important position in the world. She soon remarried, and allowed Theodore to be taken south to stay with his grandfather at Gorhambury.

Theodore's early years were nomadic. Flora's second husband was a Macgregor with an estate in the vicinity of John O'Groats. Her firstborn sometimes visited there, but she was busily having more babies, and his nanny did not hit it off with hers. Occasionally Flora was allowed to return to Mallochstrane and be with her Widell child in her former marital home. Twice, Willy Macgregor permitted her to cross the border and go to be with her Sassenach relations in the wilds of England. Mostly, Theodore lived with Geordie Gorham – that is, he spent his days and nights with Nanny Tilyard and often had tea with his grandfather.

He learned to speak without delay and was soon a conversationalist. His fairy stories were the history of the family. He was tickled to hear that he was descended from a baby in a bag swinging from the branch of a tree in the Forest of Woody.

'Which tree, Grandpa?' he asked.

'I don't know. I expect it's been cut down by now.'

'Where's the bag, Grandpa?'

'It's gone west.'

'Where's that?'

'I mean we don't have it.'

'Where did the baby come from?'

'From under a gooseberry bush.'

'Was it a gooseberry bush in the Forest?'

'In fact it was just a bush, not a gooseberry one.'

'I'd like to see it, Grandpa.'

'No doubt you will one day.'

'That baby had my name, didn't he?'

'He did – you're called Theodore after him, and because I think you're lucky too.'

'How, Grandpa?'

'We're all lucky to be born, they say.'

'We're not lucky to die, are we?'

'That depends.'

'Daddy died. Was he lucky?'

'Eat your tea, child.'

He did as he was told. Although clever at guessing the degree of awkwardness of his questions, he was always willing to desist from asking them.

One afternoon he queried: 'You've got a wife, Grandpa, haven't you?'

'I have.'

'What's her name?'

'Her Christian name is Helen.'

'What must I call her?'

'She's your step-grandmother. You'd better call her Granny.'

'Why doesn't she live with you?'

'She lives in London with my daughters, your aunts, Aunt Sybil and Aunt Sophia.'

'Don't any of them come and see you?'

'I go to see them from time to time.'

'Are they happy without you, Grandpa?'

'I believe so.'

'Are you happy without them?'

'I'd be happier if you talked less and ate more of your tea.'

At the age of six Theodore fell ill with whooping cough. He grew iller and weaker, and Geordie was increasingly distressed. He informed Flora, who hurried south. What struck everybody who attended the bed of sickness was the dignity of the boy even when he was coughing his heart out and crying. At length the crisis subsided and the danger passed. Flora had to leave Gorhambury to give birth to yet another Macgregor. Theodore recuperated slowly, and, when spring came, Geordie rented a house at Bude on the Devon Coast and sent him there in charge of Nanny Tilyard.

Theodore benefited from the breezes wafted across the Atlantic Ocean. Geordie, when he came down for visits, was glad to see the colour reappearing in the boy's cheeks. Grandfather and grandson had further conversation beside the sea.

One day Theodore asked: 'Am I lucky to be alive?'

'You are, and so are we not to have lost you.'

'Why, Grandpa?'

'Oh well, lots of reasons, but especially because you're our white hope.'

'What's that?'

'You'll be Lord Gorham when you lose me. If you and I were both dead and gone, your Aunt Sybil would inherit, and then her children, and even possibly your Aunt Sophia.'

'Can Aunt Sybil be a lord?'

'To all intents and purposes, yes.'

'But she's a lady.'

'So they say. Don't worry your head! The point is you'd be the best person to follow me and take charge of everything.'

'What's everything?'

'Gorhambury and Gorham, Goatacre and Woodhouse, and the Forest of Woody and Mallochstrane, and the land and the treasure.'

'Where's the treasure?'

'It's what we own that can't be seen, money, for example.'

'Is there a lot of money?'

'Enough.'

'Oh.'

'Don't you like the idea?'

'What idea, Grandpa?'

'Nothing – don't worry. You'll be a rich man one day, and a lord and master, but I'd like you to be better than that, outstanding, head and shoulders above the crowd. If possible, dear boy, bring a little renown to our name – it's about time. Oh well, you've done nicely so far, and I'll have to make do with you and be thankful.'

Theodore either then or later referred to the name he bore.

'You know how it's spelt, Grandpa?'

'I do indeed.'

'Why do you say a little Wi and a big dell?'

'It wasn't always said in that way. How would you say it, Theodore?'

The boy smiled, watched his grandfather's face, hesitated, and eventually replied: 'I can't.'

'It used to be Widdle,' Geordie volunteered.

They exchanged a glance, and Theodore laughed out loud, and his grandfather joined in.

Fifteen years later Theodore, 8th Lord Gorham, was a grandee, an active Parliamentarian, the cynosure of debutantes and their mothers, loaded with academic honours and generally held to be a coming man.

But he was unmarried. His lack of a wife, or of a recognised mistress, began to be the subject of gossip. He talked to the opposite sex easily, with charm and humour, accepted invitations from ladies with daughters, danced delightfully, and caused many a feminine heart to flutter. Yet at a certain point in his relations with representatives of the opposite sex he seemed to turn to stone.

His career likewise. He suffered from a form of inertia. He did not see things through. He was not living up to his promise. He was all veneer – he lacked bottom – it was a pity.

He surprised everyone by becoming engaged to The Honourable Amelia McQuarrie, one of the daughters of a peer lurking in the Scottish backwoods, Lord Benochdhu. She was nineteen, and was making a name for herself with her blackest hair and bluest eyes, and her outrageous behaviour. During the London 'season' of festivities, Lord and Lady Benochdhu, who were compared by one of their critics to a brace of shot grouse, were unaccustomed to staying up late and left Amelia to find her own way home from balls and nocturnal activities. The unsupervised girl flirted, was said to be fast, offended other girls by stealing their boyfriends and distracting their fiancés, and was raucous and rude to the older generation.

Theodore set his heart on her without delay. She accepted his proposal, and announced publicly that she had to relieve her parents of the cost of feeding her. She also said he was the best available match, and she intended to reconstruct him into a human being. They were poles apart; but she must have sent out a signal too strong for him to ignore or resist. She hacked her way through his reserve, and amused him.

Their first child looked like a Widell, but their second was the image of a friend of theirs, Angus Fitzarthur, who had straw-coloured hair and a dimpled jaw, and the third was Middle-Eastern in appearance. Her ladyship was generous, guests filled the bedrooms of Gorhambury, and the house was often shaken to its foundations by the dancing of reels into the small hours of morning. The Gorhams' servants were replaced regularly. Christmas and Easter were celebrated in almost pagan style. The neighbours were shocked, and the Vicar of St Mary's in Gorham remonstrated with his lordship.

Theodore rebuked Amelia and she tossed her head. She would accuse him of being perfect. She called him Squaretoes, a pet name for Puritans. They were heard to quarrel and shout, and according to rumour she slapped his handsome face or tried to. But they laughed and loved each other in their fashions. He benefited from the marriage in one way, as she did in another.

The benefit for Theodore was that at thirty he resigned himself to being cuckolded and subjected to a variety of indignities, and settled for melancholy, which suited him. He saw the world anew through spectacles that were the opposite of rose-coloured. He had no more illusions, he hoped for nothing much, and noticed an improvement in his powers of concentration. He moved out of the shadow of others' expectations, and was no longer inhibited by having to fulfil his promise.

He never regretted Amelia, he would not have

stooped to blame even if he had felt like blaming her: he was proud of having spotted the strange favour she could, would and did grant him. Melancholy is a misunderstood state of mind: it is often constructive, a remedy, a panacea for the person who has everything.

He performed his duties as a magnate in the country, and legislated for the common good in town, without impatience, without thinking he might be doing something more useful or agreeable elsewhere. He took time to be efficient. He was relieved to find a compartment of his life from which Amelia, her antics and accomplices, were excluded. His detachment withstood her provocations. He was not afraid to tell her the truth and be stormed at. He was becoming one of those gentlemen of an always older school, confident, composed, courteous, faintly amused by the follies and vanities of the passing show.

The bones of matrimonial contention were not sex. She was stimulated by nothing but novelty, and he had settled by now for her occasional brisk gifts of herself. He had realised that jealousy was a lost cause, and confined his comments on her extramarital activities to mild requests: 'Spare my blushes, my dear...' Meals for two were a rarity in the Gorhams' homes. She was not awake when he breakfasted, and at lunch and dinner there were usually guests. Moreover, each of them at other times of day had more interesting things to do than to sit and be scolded. But sometimes pain took precedence over pleasure.

Theodore would say: 'You have not set foot in Gorhambury for a fortnight, and the children miss you even if I do not.'

'I bore them, now they bore me, they're such frightful bores,' she might retort, or say, 'Absence makes their little hearts grow fonder.'

'One day you'll pay for having been a bad mother.'

'Fiddlesticks! I refuse to be anybody's slave. You should know that, Theodore.'

And she would tell him to sell a farm so that she could buy a frock or give another party.

Their reconciliations were on the rueful side. He would say: 'You're a brick wall, Amelia, and I'm not butting my head against it any more,' and she would echo: 'You're a skinflint, a skinflint without a spark.'

Nevertheless, as time went on, they each realised, whether or not they admitted, Theodore that Amelia was a star shedding its light upon him, and Amelia that Theodore was more honest and good than other men.

His qualities were not overlooked by the wider world. He turned out to be a born chairman, and had innumerable directorships. Every organisation seemed to want him to be its treasurer. He served on committees set up by the House of Lords, and volunteered to do research for the speechmakers.

In the later eighteen-thirties a national row erupted over the so-called People's Charter. It was a liberalising document, not particularly radical, and was supported by the beneficiaries of the new industrial order, the better off and better educated artisans and workers. Parliament ignored it. The Chartist leaders were moderate men. But an Irishman called Feargus O'Connor stepped in, roused the rabble, issued threats of 'physical force', and was involved in riots in Newport.

The Establishment picked Theodore to defuse the situation. He did so in record time. The Chartist movement ceased to trouble the body politic, and eventually its aims were enshrined in the constitution.

Theodore had met Mr O'Connor, whose staple topic of conversation was blue murder. He acted on his experience of the Irish character, with its two great loves, of violence and horses. Having listened to Mr O'Connor, he invited him to stay at Gorhambury and hunt with the Gorhambury Hounds. The Irishman spent several days on the backs of Theodore's splendid hunters, hoping to do violence to foxes. As a result he was accused of selling out to the aristocracy, thus compromising his credibility as a champion of the people.

Theodore was more in demand owing to his success in subduing the Chartists. His opinion was sought by men of power, he wielded influence in his back room, and was ever willing, self-effacing, and dependable. That he was known to be married to a difficult wife protected him from some of the darts of envy and spite.

Inevitably, he was drawn into the team assembled by Prince Albert to assist with the creation of the Great Exhibition of 1851. He was called upon to take care of the trees in the part of Hyde Park unconnected with the Exhibition. Then he was given a watching brief on the drainage from the public lavatories. He sat on several committees, one to choose the art to be exhibited, another to decide on the flooring that would be trodden by millions of feet, a third and a fourth to make sure of available First Aid.

One day he received an invitation to lunch with Sir Ralph Houghton, a former equerry to Queen Victoria and now one of Prince Albert's private secretaries. Sir Ralph was involved, as Theodore was, in the preparations for the Exhibition; they were also friendly acquaintances. Towards the end of the meal their conversation took a personal turn.

'Lord Gorham, I understand that your family has had dealings with royalty in the distant past.'

'Two members of my family, Sir Ralph, one of whom became the first baron,' Theodore replied.

'The second member being the elegant wife of the future baron?'

'Precisely. King Charles the Second spent a night at Gorhambury.'

'Ah.'

'He arrived late and left early, according to family records, and repaid my forefather by ennobling him.'

'Kings are busy. I'm sure King Charles had other fish to fry, if you'll pardon the expression. But he was a generous potentate, and appreciative of generosity.'

'I could not quarrel with your description, Sir Ralph.'

'Well now, I invoked history before asking if you had met our Queen or her Consort?'

'I have not had that pleasure.'

Sir Ernest cleared his throat.

'Pleasure possibly, privilege yes,' he said, and continued: 'Her Majesty will be visiting the Exhibition on several occasions, and it's been decided in high places that you would be her ideal guide.'

'I'm honoured, Sir Ralph, but surely she will be accompanied by her husband and by Paxton? They built the place and know it inside out.'

'They will be preoccupied. Her Majesty is a wonderful woman, but no doubt a gentleman-in-waiting would be of assistance socially and to make sure that she shook deserving hands, don't you know?'

'I do, and shall, of course, be only too happy to serve the Queen.'

Accordingly, Lord and Lady Gorham were bidden to join the royal party for the ceremony of declaring the Exhibition open. Amelia accepted for both of them, but cried off in a tantrum at the last minute and Theodore went alone.

He was introduced to Queen Victoria, a small but authoritative woman aged thirty-two, who said to him: 'Where's your wife?'

'Resting, Ma'am. She has been unwell. She sends Your Majesty her deepest regrets and apologies.'

The Queen sniffed and muttered as she moved away: 'Unwell, is it?'

His second meeting with her was not more profitable from any point of view. For one thing, she was surrounded by guides and assistants and he felt superfluous, for another she picked on his name, his titular name, Gorham, thankfully not the old family surname, and seemed to take exception to it.

'What's the correct pronunciation?' she began.

'Well, Ma'am, in the country they accentuate the second syllable – they breed pigs and dream of ham down there – but in London it's apt to become one syllable, "Gorm", because townees have no time for two syllables.'

This humorous speech was greeted with a grunt, intentionally or unintentionally porcine.

During further visits the Queen had fewer attendants and Theodore had more responsibilities. He was impressed by her regality, but could not help noticing that she was not always strong on diplomacy. He became adept at filling silences and supplying a few comforting words.

A typical example was her encounter with Mr Stevenson, a miller from Yorkshire, who was showing his machine for producing flour of different qualities for making bread. He explained its workings, and that it replaced windmills and millstones, at some length.

When the Queen could get a word in edgeways she remarked: 'Beastly weather we're having.'

Mr Stevenson looked flummoxed, but recovered his poise and produced a plate on which were arranged slivers of white bread and butter and slivers of coarse brown.

'You take a big bite of these, Your Majesty, and you'll see what I've been driving at,' he said.

She looked at Theodore and asked: 'Must I?'

'A nibble, Ma'am,' he suggested.

'You do the nibbling,' she replied.

He had to say to Mr Stevenson: 'Her Majesty wishes me to taste your bread. Would you mind?'

'That's not the same thing at all,' Mr Stevenson protested, flushing dark red.

'It's a royal command,' Theodore warned.

'Oh well, you eat some, whoever you are.'

Theodore did so, first the white, then the brown. While he munched the latter, the Queen said to Mr Stevenson: 'That bread looks heavy.'

'It is heavy, it's the staff of life, Your Majesty, the white's reserved for weak stomachs.'

'I eat white bread,' she divulged, moving on to the next exhibit.

Theodore, in order to console or pacify Mr Stevenson, had to go back and pretend that Her Majesty would like to have one of his white loaves to eat with her breakfast.

He had to be diplomatic on other days. The representative of a British colony in the Pacific Ocean approached the Queen with his hat on, a sort of bowler with feathers sticking up at the back. He smiled toothily and extended both his hands in a warm greeting. The Queen, instead of taking his hands, turned her back and said to Theodore: 'Tell him to take his hat off!'

'The gentleman's wearing it out of respect, Ma'am. The hat is a sign of respect in his country – it's on his head to honour you,' Theodore informed her.

She relented and had the grace to greet her subject, but chose to explain her previous reaction thus: 'Your hat gave me a fright.'

Sometimes Her Majesty was not in a talkative mood, and Theodore had to speak for her, as if she had been his dummy. Her visits to the Exhibition were frequent, and signalled her pride in the achievement of Prince Albert. She usually brought along Ladies-in-Waiting, who lurked nervously in the background, and on one or two occasions her children, who also looked nervous. Theodore understood why: Her Majesty's silences could be oppressive, and her way of calling a spade a spade disconcerting. On being presented with a portrayal of the royal arms in pokerwork she opined, 'Ugly thing!'

On several afternoons she consented to take tea in a room set aside for her refreshment, and Theodore would be seated beside her. Their conversation was always limited. She asked if he had children, and, before he could answer, if he had dogs. She smiled on being told that he was the owner of a forest called Woody. She might eat a small sandwich very slowly: which verified the rumour that she claimed to chew every mouthful fifty or sixty times. She expressed a wish to meet Lady Gorham.

Amelia was prevailed upon to behave herself for a change, and Theodore effected the introduction.

The Queen remarked: 'We were sorry not to see you before, Lady Gorham.'

'I am the sorry one, Your Majesty.'

'We hope you are healthier now.'

'I'm better, Ma'am.'

'So you should be, with such an agreeable husband.'

Amelia did not answer back, she had met her match and looked crushed.

'Goodbye,' the Queen said sternly.

Amelia mumbled thanks and receded into the crowd, while Theodore continued to perform his duties.

The side of the Queen that was not stern, stuffy, taciturn and tactless, evinced itself more often the more time they spent together. She had a sudden smile that lit her face as if from within. One afternoon she amazed him by revealing that she was capable of a giggle. There were not only sparrows within the confines of the Great Exhibition, but also pigeons, one of which defecated from above on to Theodore's jacket. Her Majesty was much amused, pointed to the faecal blob on his shoulder, warned him that it was acid and would burn a hole, and indicated that her Ladies-in-Waiting were at liberty to be reduced to fits.

She bade Theodore a goodbye that was appreciative when the doors of the Exhibition were closed, and a few weeks later he received a letter from the Earl Marshal, the Duke of Norfolk, announcing that Queen Victoria had granted him the additional title of Marquess and in future would address him formally as 'Our right trusty and entirely beloved cousin'.

Amelia teased him. She called him *Monsieur le Marquis*, and said that a Marchioness was a mouthful. She said she had only at last come to terms with bearing children who were meant to be honourable, and now she had to adjust to their being lordlings and ladyships. It was very hard on her, she grumbled, however nice it was for him. She swore she would disown her marriage and travel incognito as Miss Woody.

None of it was true. She had been joking, she assured Theodore in private. The title was for once deserved, she said; and a majority of outsiders agreed with her.

Theodore was to be the Marquess of Gorhambury; and the pronunciation of the word was ruled to be now and in future 'Gormbury'. He would continue to bear his former title as well, Lord Gorham, and the eldest of his three sons, Claud, was granted usage of a courtesy title, Lord Bushton.

Just as money is said to attract money in the matrimonial context, so one honour attracts more. Theodore became a Privy Counsellor, then a Knight-Commander of the Order of St Michael and St George, then a Doctor of Literature although he was not a literary man, then a

136

Deputy Lord Lieutenant of his country; and his full mode of address was The Right Honourable The Marquess of Gormbury, PC, KCMG, D.Litt., DL. The price of such trinkets, he discovered, was to have to redouble his services to the community. He became a Lord-in-Waiting to the Monarch and had to attend all royal functions. He was fagged relentlessly by his fellow peers in the House of Lords. He had more duties in the City of London, and in the country. He was on the treadmill of success.

The Gorhamburys changed places geographically. Theodore lived mostly in the metropolis, Amelia in their country seat. She was now in her forties and seemed to have lost interest in romance; and as ladies in retirement are apt to amuse themselves with either art or sport, she spent her winters in the hunting field and expressed her artistic self by redesigning the Gorhambury gardens in spring and summer. Theodore, meanwhile, was in London, or at Windsor or Balmoral, or traipsing to outlandish places to receive a prize or a plaudit for having done what it was in his nature to do.

He had to have an office in his house in Westminster, and employ a permanent secretary to deal with his diary and correspondence. She was a middle-aged widow with common sense, Mrs Peters, who exerted a calming influence over his hectic weekdays. She also helped him to recuperate from weekends spent with Amelia and her guests. His wife still had the power to upset him.

He was in his Smith Square house when the telegram arrived to state that her ladyship was in Gorham Cottage Hospital following a fall out hunting. He was annoyed. He showed it to Mrs Peters, and instructed her to cancel several of his engagements. He caught his train and recollected all the times he had ordered, asked, begged Amelia to stop hunting. She was a reckless rider and prone to falling off. She liked reckless horses, between them they took crazy risks, and one or the other or both often came to grief. Theodore did not care deeply whether she lived or died, but dreaded the complications of her disabling herself.

He went straight to the hospital. Doctors and nurses greeted him with grave faces. Amelia had broken her back. He entered her room. She lay rigidly in bed, only her white face with eyes closed showing. Sadness took over from anger in his heart. He stood beside the bed, looking down on her, not sure she was alive although the Matron had said she was. He raised his hand and with difficulty, in case he disturbed her, and because he had not touched her for so long, laid it on her forehead.

After a moment, without opening her eyes, she whispered: 'Theodore?'

'Yes,' he said.

'You told me so.'

'Yes.'

'Go away, lead your life! I'll try to get better. Do you hear me?'

'Yes.'

138

'Promise!'

'Yes.'

She said no more. He was hoping to have the chance to be comforting, and to utter more than monosyllables. Some time elapsed, and the Matron led him out of Amelia's presence.

He stayed at Gorhambury for several days. But he was not good at coping with the children, and, when he revisited the hospital, Amelia was not pleased with him for breaking his promise. He returned to Smith Square, and with Mrs Peters, when he was telling her the news, he cried.

He had not cried since he was a child. It was very awkward: he sobbed behind his desk, she sat on the other side, and he was apologising and she was saying she understood and was sorry, and he could not stop.

At last he controlled himself and wiped his eyes.

'Are you all right, sir?' Mrs Peters asked.

He shook his head.

She again professed to understand.

'No, you don't, you can't,' he replied. 'It's my marriage.'

She waited.

'It was so complicated,' he said. 'And now we can't make sense of it.'

Mrs Peters remained silent.

'I've never talked to anyone about my marriage. Do you mind? I know I can trust you.'

'I don't mind, and I wouldn't ever let you down, sir.'

'There's really nothing to say. But it's good for me to know I could confide in you. Thank you so much.'

'I was married too, Lord Gorhambury.'

'Of course, of course you were. What a strange relationship!'

'Yes indeed – yes.'

They left it at that. Their exchanges had been more intimate than the words, or the scenario, suggested. Which relationship was stronger, his with Amelia or his with Mrs Peters, was never clear; but he and his secretary were not shy with each other after his tears and their subsequent exchanges. In the ensuing days and weeks Theodore was grateful for his secretary's company and composure.

Amelia weakened. Too much of her was paralysed, and her life was proving to be insupportable. Theodore watched over her from afar – he was sent packing if he tried to sit with or even see her. He knew she did it for his sake, and he was touched that she should think he cared for her so little that he could resume his customary pursuits; but he played her game and pretended in notes and messages to be carrying on as before. He stayed mainly in London, marking time.

At last he was summoned to her bedside. The high-spirited girl he had married, naughty, funny, had become a white bony mask with huge eyes.

She said to him slowly and faintly: 'I didn't mean to bother you.'

He replied that she had not.

But she persisted: 'I've bothered you enough without all this.'

He replied: 'I wouldn't have done anything if you hadn't bothered me.'

She flickered her eyelids negatively.

'Thanks for a lovely time,' she said.

They did not speak for a moment.

'Sorry to leave you with Claud and the others.'

'Do you want to see them?'

'No. We've not been perfect parents.'

'No.'

After another pause she said: 'Remember me as I was. I didn't want you to see me as I am.'

'I'm glad to be seeing you, Amelia.'

'*Au revoir*,' she whispered, and closed her eyes and seemed to sleep. In due course he tiptoed out of the room. A few days later she died.

Claud, Lord Bushton, was nineteen years of age, coarse-grained and rumbustious, very different from his parents with whom he was never close – and vice versa. Theodore let him rule the roost at Gorhambury and spent his declining years almost exclusively in his house in Smith Square. He resigned from one of his posts after another and at last succeeded in persuading Queen Victoria that he was no longer fit for the demanding rituals of the Court.

Two years after Amelia's death he invited Mrs Peters to share his home. They were happy together, although he never called her by her first name and she always called him Lord Gorhambury.

Two and Three

The motto of the family, coined during the reign of King Charles the Second, was another of the far-fetched puns affected by old-style heraldry. It read 'Widel and wealth,' but could look even more boastful: 'Wide land wealth.' Theodore had changed it to 'Wide interests and sympathies.' But Claud, formerly Lord Bushton, now second Marquess of Gorhambury and ninth Baron Gorham, reverted to the original: he put it on his writing paper under an embossed coronet.

Claud inherited the title in his thirty-first year. He had married a local girl by then, Matilda Stephens, who was a bovine type. They had already produced a son and heir presumptive, Arthur, Lord Bushton. Claud and Matilda, having lived in modest circumstances – a house round by the stables, an allowance from his father that they considered measly – celebrated the fact that their long wait was over and they were rich. Claud insisted on moving into Gorhambury later in the day on which his father died in London. On the same day he was telling his head groom that as soon as the blasted funeral was over he was off to buy racehorses in Newmarket.

He was not ageing well. The freckle-faced

red-haired boy with a forelock had grown into a top-heavy man, who had hands like hams with brown spots on the back, a greedy look in his eye and a short temper. What had become of his breeding? There was no trace in him of either his father's capability and melancholy charm or his mother's rebellious gaiety. No Widell so boorish figured in the family history. The assumption had to be that he resembled unknown ancestors dead and buried for centuries, a Scottish cut-throat or a parent willing to leave his or her baby dangling from the branch of a forest tree.

Breakfast in the Banqueting Hall of Gorhambury was no longer a lesson in aristocratic etiquette. Gone were the eggs boiled or poached, the triangles of toast, the perfumed tea and the fruits from the garden in season. In their place were red meat, steaks and chops, claret and brandy. The Marquess at the head of the refectory table manipulated his knife and fork with his elbows sticking out, and the Marchioness sat at the other end, flabby and amiable, continuing as if to chew the cud after she had finished eating. Usually there were guests between them, good sports with bleary eyes who engaged in competitions with their host to see who could swallow most food and drink, and a few women cringing round their hostess. But occasionally the Gorhamburys were alone, and their versions of conversation would fill an hour or more of meal-time.

Claud would say: 'We're hunting at Goatacre today – Meet's at The Goat.'

Matilda would answer in due course: 'That's nice.'

Another pause ensued, punctuated by the clangs and squeaks of His Lordship's eating irons, and his eructations of wind.

Then Claud would again toss the ball into the air.

'Where's the boy?'

'Upstairs,' says Matilda.

Another break for the consumption of victuals.

'What's for supper?'

'Venison, dear.'

Claud picked his teeth, blew his nose explosively, stood up, passed more wind, and shouted at his better half: 'I'll be bringing home a dozen or so for the venison.'

The single feature that could be said almost to redeem Claud was his appreciation of a fine fast horse. He loved racehorses, insofar as he loved anything. In his muddled way he might have loved the aristocratic qualities of such beasts that were lacking in himself. He bought them and bet on them to win him races. He spent a mounting proportion of family funds on pricey horseflesh, and was not interested in being paid or repaid for his pleasure. He was glad to be a Marquess able to stand and stare at a perfectly-made animal in his stablcyard or galloping at full tilt to glory on a racecourse.

He was bad at business, and a bad landlord. He sacked people who told him things he did not want to hear, and employed agreeable types who stole from him. He enjoyed other sports when he was not racing: blood sports. Occasionally, when he had not drunk more liquor than he could hold, he put Matilda in the family way.

Every sensible person said that it, and he, could not last. The consensus was that Claud would blow up, for he was growing fatter daily, and that his son Arthur was the better man. But the strenuous exercise, the falls out hunting, the mishaps with shotguns, and the roistering night after night, went on for nearly ten years.

Claud's end was called poetic justice by some, and by others a joke.

The season was winter. The Marquess had been hunting with his hounds and had invited about twenty-four cronies, all in their breeches and boots, back to Gorhambury for an evening meal. The company was more numerous than Matilda and her servants were expecting, there were shortages of food, livestock had to be fetched and butchered, and as a result the gentlemen partook of much liquid refreshment while they waited. To while away the time Claud organised games – shove ha'penny, carpet bowls, the three card trick and blackjack – and began to keep a tally of winners. Two teams were then formed of about ten men apiece, one captained by Claud and the other by Captain Duplock, a retired cavalry officer who had a property over at West Ashe.

The competitive inclinations of the sportsmen were inflamed by the alcohol in their empty stomachs. Arguing commenced and high words were spoken. Claud was keeping the score on a scrap of paper: under two headings, For me and For you, he made crosses with the stump of a lead pencil. At a certain moment the hubbub of rallying cries, congratulations, curses and guffaws of laughter were stilled by a loud voice and an alarming statement.

'My lord! My lord, you are playing fast and loose with the score.'

A hush fell slowly. Claud, purple in the face and with popping eyes, was confronted by Captain Duplock, mustached, looking as if he were made of steel and leather, and bristling.

'You are putting our crosses in the list of yours,' the Captain said.

'Balderdash!' Claud expostulated.

'Excuse me, my lord, your team is winning when it should be losing.'

Partisan shouts broke out.

'Mind your language, sir,' Claud yelled. 'I won't stand for insolence.'

Another man intervened, Lionel Trubbington, Claud's friend and the Field Master of the Gorhambury Hounds.

'Let Captain Duplock keep the score – we'll have his blood if he makes a mistake.'

Voices agreed with this suggestion.

Claud threw his paper and pencil on to the floor, and waddled off muttering, 'Where the hell is our supper?'

Laughter glossed over the episode. Supper was served. But the teams managed to stay separate at table, and Claud, having been heard to say

147

before he sat down 'Keep the twister well away from me', directed dirty looks at Captain Duplock throughout the meal.

The games resumed immediately afterwards. More alcohol had translated competitiveness into hostility. Tempers were soon lost. Again, a louder exclamation, a roar, interrupted the proceedings.

Claud shouted at Captain Duplock: 'You're the cheat!'

'You are drunk, my lord. If you were not drunk, I would slap your face,' the Captain retorted.

'Don't worry,' said Claud. 'I'll save you the trouble – here, take that!' He was clumsily assaulting Captain Duplock, who parried the blows and called on Mr Trubbington to take the Marquess to bed.

'Captain Dublock,' Claud began with as much dignity as he could muster.

'Duplock,' several people corrected him.

'Well – whatever you call yourself – I demand satisfaction, sir.'

'You are in no state to fight a duel, Lord Gorhambury. I urge you to go to bed.'

'I'm not so drunk that I can't shoot a cock sparrow at fifty yards. Get my guns, somebody!'

Calls for restraint and pleas for peace were heard. But a mischief-maker is always on hand to fan a flame. The gun-case was placed on the refectory table. Claud opened it and started to assemble the two guns it contained. Mr Trubbington and others did their best to halt the rush towards danger, and were opposed by

148

the cheers and jeers of the members of the Duplock team.

Claud led an exodus out of doors and into the park. It was a moonlit night – 'Bright enough', he said. He handed one loaded gun to Captain Duplock, forced the Captain physically and with accusations of cowardice to take it, and marched away, counting his steps. At a distance of fifty yards he turned round and, even though the crowd now begged for reason to prevail as they retreated from the firing line, called across the open space.

'Can you see and hear me, Captain Duplock?'

'My lord, this charade has gone too far.'

'Exactly, Captain – you've gone too far – that's why you're now about to meet your maker.'

'My lord, I retract any offence I may have given. We were playing games. I wish to return to my wife and my home.'

'Too far and too late, Captain Duplock!'

The Captain appealed for help, but Claud threatened to shoot anyone who obstructed the proceedings. Mr Trubbington was telling him not to murder the Captain or anybody else. Claud slurred an ultimate threat.

'When I've counted up to fifteen we are both allowed to fire.'

'Lord Gorhambury, I will not shoot you,' Captain Duplock returned, and with that he pointed his gun heavenwards and fired both barrels, from which fiery flashes issued.

Claud counted quickly up to fifteen, the Captain dropped the gun, turned his back and sank on to his knees, and the other gun exploded. Claud had shot Captain Duplock – luckily in the buttocks and the wounds were skin deep. But people, particularly the members of the Captain's team, thought they had seen their leader shot in cold blood. Angrily, drunkenly, they ran towards Claud, bellowing vengeful cries. He in his turn dropped his gun and took to his heels, as the saying euphemistically puts it: in fact he waddled and wobbled in an attempt to escape, and was laughing – he seemed to think he had done something funny. In the dark he tripped or slipped – the park was full of cowpats – and fell heavily. When his pursuers, his hunters, caught up with him, he was dead.

Arthur Widell, third Marquess of Gorhambury and tenth Lord Gorham, bore some resemblances to his father, Crackpot Claud, as the second Marquess had been known locally. Arthur, too, was tall and big-boned; but he had a more violent temper, and, as if to balance its uncontrollability, a strong sense of fair play. The consequential problems began to plague him at boarding school. In rough games he would lose his temper and hurt boys, occasionally boys smaller and weaker than he was, and then suffer regrets and remorse. On the other hand he also lost his temper with bullies, big bullies who hit him harder than he could hit them or else would formally beat him. He was admired by some for his practical attitude to justice, but feared by others, and the larger he grew the greater the number of the others.

His boyhood and youth at Gorhambury were pleasant. His mother, Matilda, was vastly relieved to be a widow, and content to be lazy. He had two ugly sisters who doted on him, Clarissa and Phoebe, and two much younger brothers, David and William. Although David was cleverer than he was, and William was better-looking, Arthur was undisputed leader of the pack of his siblings, and not only because he was the Marquess and they were his understudies.

He seemed to have been born to command, and therefore got on well with his servants: he and they knew at once where they stood in a hierarchical sense, and friendly relations resulted so long as the rules were kept. He was respect-ful of the respect he received, considerate and generous, but hard on disloyalty or dis-honesty, and he inspired a healthy terror of his temper.

He met the rest of the world – equals, superiors, strangers, members of the opposite sex – with an open regard if not exactly an open mind, for he was conventional and conservative. He had dignity. He could be insensitive. He could be brutal. He was never a bad boy, and he became a decent man of limited intelligence.

Instead of going to university he joined the army. He was meant to be a soldier for a year or two, and would then devote himself to the management of his estate and the acquittal of his duties as county bigwig and peer of the realm. But he was made for military life. He was sent to India, loved it, played polo and excelled at tent-pegging, resisted the blandishments of Asian houris and the 'fishing fleet' of English maidens, became a Major with medals, and came home in time to play his part in Queen Victoria's funeral in 1901.

He resigned his commission when he was twenty-four years old. He was set on marriage without further delay. He organised a ball at Gorhambury partly to celebrate his homecoming. The gentry from miles around attended with every possible daughter in tow. It was a glorious occasion, the great reception rooms reopened, the innumerable candles in the chandeliers lit, flowers everywhere, the spare bedrooms occupied by brother officers with and without wives, and the host in the blue evening uniform he was still allowed to wear.

He stood with his mother, sisters and brothers at the doorway into the staircase hall, greeting his guests, and music from the drawing-room cleared for dancing mingled with the scents of flowers. By the time he had shaken the last hand, he had chosen. He approached her in the anteroom and asked if she would do him the honour of being his partner in the first dance. She overcame her shyness and scruples, and they danced together and alone for several minutes until other couples took to the floor.

She was Miss Jemima Foster, eighteen and a neighbour – her father was an impoverished squire over in the Foxham direction. Arthur wished to make her his Marchioness because she had no powerful relations and no money to be wilful with, was too young to be soiled, well-covered physically, not a clothes-horse, had a wide smile and what looked like child-bearing hips.

His courtship was of a type that might be called military or agricultural. He said to her even as they finished dancing: 'I knew you were the one for me.' She had been heating up throughout the evening, by the excitement of her first ball, by being singled out by the big important personage who was giving it, by being trundled round the dance floor in front of everyone and by knowing how she would be criticised and envied, and now she boiled – she was overcome by embarrassment and alarm: what was he saying, what did he mean? She thanked him and had to be escorted to the ladies' cloak-room by her mother. They decided that the Marquess had only referred to their temporary partnership.

Arthur asked her for two more dances in the course of the extended evening. He held Jemima at arm's length and showed no emotion, apart from perspiring freely. But a week later Anthony Foster Esquire received a letter from Gorhambury, in which Arthur stated that he would call at the Fosters' home at four p.m. on such and such a day to speak privately to Mr Foster, unless informed that the date and time were incon-venient. It caused considerable panic. Jemima had three sisters, one older, Anne, two younger, Marion and Michaela: they all suffered from vapours. Mr Foster ruled that it could do no harm to allow the Marquess to have his say, which might refer to unromantic matters.

Arthur asked for Jemima's hand in marriage. Mr Foster said he had no objection in principle, and would let Jemima answer for herself. Jemima was summoned into her father's study, told the news, and left alone with her suitor. They stood at some distance from each other, both bright red in the face, she hanging her head.

'You would honour me and please me by agreeing to be my wife,' he said after clearing his throat loudly. 'I would take good care of you.'

She replied: 'Thank you, sir. You are most kind. But you do not know me.'

'I know my own mind.'

'Well – I do not know you.'

'There's not a lot to know. I'm a plain man. You have danced with me.'

'I am very young, sir.'

'Not for long.'

'I have my sisters to consider.'

'What have your sisters got to do with it? I can't marry them, too.'

'No, sir.' She giggled nervously. 'But I don't want them to feel left out.'

'And I don't know what you're talking about. My dear girl, you haven't answered my question. I'd be a faithful husband – there's a lot of dog in me.'

She giggled again and replied: 'You are offering me a life above my station.'

'I don't want hoity-toitiness.'

'You will want an heir, sir, and I may not be able to provide one.'

'We could have a shot at it, and cross bridges when we come to them.'

'Oh sir, I'm not sure, I'm frightened to hear you put it that way.'

'Apologies – I meant no harm. I hope you'd grow used to me. I'm not asking for more than that.'

'You're modest, sir.'

'I've nothing much to be proud of.'

'Sir, I see how straightforward you are, and I have no doubt that you're wiser as well as older and more experienced than I am. Please tell me how I am to respond to your proposal.'

'Damme, that's a new twist!'

'Have I said something wrong?'

'No, no, my dear. Most girls wouldn't give a fellow who was courting her the right to settle her fate. Don't worry! I've thought things over, and my advice is that you might as well say yes. You'd have a roof over your head and four square meals a day with me. I'm not a lover-boy, if that's what you're looking for.'

'I'm not.'

'What's it to be then?'

She hesitated before whispering: 'I'll do as I'm told.'

'Thank you, thank you,' he barked in a distinctly canine manner.

He approached her and, holding her firmly by the shoulders in his outstretched arms, kissed her on the top of her head.

The Marquess of Gorhambury married Miss Jemima Foster, and at last, after numerous 'bosh shots' in his terminology, the union was consummated. In the fullness of time a son was born, Valentine Theodore. And the popular assumption was that the cup of the Widells overflowed with every worldly privilege and joy.

It was not like that. Jemima had a grand husband who bestowed upon her a grand title. She discovered that he was fond, and often touching. She had more money than she could have spent even if she had been a spendthrift. She had expensive clothes, and a strong room full of jewellery she was entitled to wear. She had a town house and almost a palace in the country. She had servants galore.

But she was awestruck and she quailed.

She was in awe of her servants. Nearly all were older than she was, and the butler and cook, the housekeeper and head-groom were like her grandparents. They were nice to her, but she dared to ask them for nothing, let alone give an order; and when she fetched a spoon from the sideboard or looked for a pair of her shoes in the brushing room, she was caught out and felt like a felon.

Her sisters-in-law and brothers-in-law were less indulgent than her servants. At least she was convinced that they were. They seemed to be waiting and watching in order to gather evidence of her ignorance. They definitely delayed too long before moving with their mother into the Dower House located on the far side of the park.

When they had all cohabited for several months, Jemima grasped the facts that Clarissa and Phoebe, whose god was Arthur, thought his wife unworthy; while David and William could not bring themselves to love a woman who might, and soon threatened to, spoil their chances of wearing the coronet and hanging their names in bold print on the family tree.

As for the Dowager Marchioness, she was the opposite of an alchemist. Dim-witted and docile, living to eat apparently, she still seemed to be in charge of Gorhambury. At least she ordered the food, and the servants addressed their questions to her.

Moreover, Arthur seemed oblivious of Jemima's difficulties, not to be on her side, and was unapproachable.

Then a dramatic change for the worse occurred in the early days of her pregnancy. Jemima had suffered few adverse symptoms of her condition, the only inconvenient one was that her temperature refused to stabilise. Arthur was excited by the prospect of fatherhood, and had been treating her like cut glass. On the relevant evening they were changing their clothes before dinner. He was donning his stiff white shirt with stick-up collar, a ritual that strained his patience, she was in their bedroom adjoining. She was overcome with heat and called to Arthur and asked him if he would open a window wide. He said he would. He tried to, but they were huge sash windows, he could not move the first one at all, and the second only six inches. She said it would do. But five minutes later her teeth were chattering, and she again summoned Arthur. He closed the window with more difficulty, and she was vaguely aware that he was having to control his irritation. When she immediately seemed to catch fire, instead of seeking help she tugged at the window herself. She was unable to shift it and was afraid that the effort might have already injured her child, therefore once more called to Arthur.

He joined her with his white tie undone. He was clearly angry, but controlled himself to the extent of saying in a voice that trembled: 'You shouldn't have, Jemima – if you're hurt I'll be most upset.' He then tackled the window. But it was stuck. He uttered a hoarse cry, combining rage, frustration, desperation, and seizing one of a pair of tall silver candlesticks on her dressing-table he began to batter the windowpanes.

She was paralysed by surprise and fear. She had never encountered or imagined such violence. He battered half a dozen windowpanes, crying out and cursing, dropped the candlestick and stumbled past Jemima, saying, 'That's what you wanted!'

He returned to his dressing-room. Now the bedroom began to fill with smoke. Against the odds the candle had fallen out of the candlestick used to break the glass, remained alight on the floor, and set fire to an old lined and interlined curtain. Jemima screamed. Arthur stormed in, looking mad with fury, staring-eyed, his lips drawn away from his teeth in a snarl, and, taking in the situation, upended her dressing-table, sending mirror, pots of cosmetics, silver-backed hairbrushes flying, tore down the curtain and stamped on it as if in a savage dance. He demanded water – 'Get me water, get it!' – and when she had complied, and he had thrown a jugful on to the smoking curtain, he threw the jug across the room, so that it shattered against the opposite wall. He was swearing, and without looking at Jemima he ran out, slamming the door that connected with his dressing-room.

She wept. She lay down on their nuptial couch and wept as she never had in her adult life. She could not control her sobbing although she knew it could be affecting her unborn child.

Half an hour passed, and he knocked on her door. He was painfully anguished, contrite, apologetic, and tried to comfort her. She sobbed out her other troubles on his shoulder, trouble with the other members of his family and his servants. He said he would see to it and begged her to rest and dine in her bedroom. She agreed, she obeyed, she was afraid of crossing him; and she forgave him verbally and they bade each other good night.

In the morning, after she had had her breakfast in bed by order of his lordship, when she went

159

downstairs at eleven o'clock, Arthur greeted her and explained that his mother and his siblings had already moved out of Gorhambury and into the Dower House, and some of the other servants had volunteered to retire – they would have cottages on the estate and respectable pensions.

Jemima was grateful – she had to be – she also realised with a shiver that she was losing five restraining influences and possible shields from the wrath of her husband.

But she was a country girl and down to earth. In time and on reflection she remembered that she had married for better or worse, and realised her marriage was indissoluble. She decided to blot out that dreadful scene, hoped it would not be repeated, was glad that Arthur had confined his assault to the furniture, and aware that she had gained an ascendancy over him. She consoled herself with appreciation of all she had received, the material and non-material gifts, his whole-heartedness and reliance upon her.

When Valentine, Lord Bushton, was born, Arthur was pleased and grateful to his wife. The shadows over the marriage deepened nonetheless. He was not so easy with Jemima as he had been: he was still ashamed of having shown her how bad his temper was. They both had regrets: Jemima was sorry to have sustained internal damage during the birth of Valentine and that she would be unable to bear any more children. He thought he was no good at public speaking, steered clear of the House of Lords, said he was useless, and that counting his money was not a fit occupation for a gentleman. He apologised to his wife for not resembling his grandfather, and she apologised for being barren – she was sorry Valentine would have no siblings to play with.

Thankfully, they were always busy, he had an estate to manage, she had a great house and an extensive garden to look after, and they had local obligations. There were no more explosions, and they rubbed along pretty well into the second decade of the twentieth century.

It was worse when it happened again. Arthur was preoccupied by the international situation and possibility of war with Germany. The family of three was having lunch together. Valentine, a pale blond boy of nine, annoyed his father by whining that he did not like and would not eat his Brussels sprouts. Arthur shouted at him to desist, Valentine cried, Arthur shouted louder, and the boy rebelled by getting off his chair and running round to be comforted by his mother. Arthur caught him by the arm, and, standing, flung him across the room so that his head crashed into a leg of the sideboard.

Harvey, the butler, and a footman called William, were close by and bent to pick up Lord Bushton, who seemed to be insensible. Arthur dismissed them: 'Go away, go!' Jemima hurried to her son. Arthur ordered her to stop, he said he was sick of her spoiling the boy – Valentine was shamming and would be all right. She disobeyed – she was almost as angry as he was. Whereupon Arthur seized her by the hair, pulled her to the ground and dragged her away, round the table, ignoring her screams. He swore at both Jemima and Valentine, he was 'teaching them a bloody lesson'; and when his wife's hair was tugged out of her scalp he kicked her, then kicked out at Valentine in passing, and rushed from the room.

Valentine was not too badly hurt after all, except in his feelings. Jemima had a lot of hair and would replace the little she had lost. But Arthur's penitence did not cut ice with his wife and son. His behaviour in front of the servants scandalised the neighbourhood. A difficult time for the Widells was interrupted by the declaration of war, and by Arthur volunteering to rejoin his regiment.

Major The Marquess of Gorhambury was in his mid-thirties, and because of his age was detailed to do a desk job behind the lines in Northern France. Before long, owing to the wastage of officers in battle, he obtained the transfer he had hoped for to active service in the trenches. The winters of 1914 and 1915 were cold and wet, the summers mainly wet. In his regiment the consensus was that they would all be stuck in their dugouts and mud until the war ended. For Arthur, modern warfare was not a patch on soldiering in India with sport and garden parties in the sunshine thrown in.

He wrote to Jemima, and she answered his letters, which were terse and sad.

'Dearest,' he wrote, 'no fun here, weather filthy, and the men glum, poor devils. Thinking always of you and Valentine. I do not deserve you. Arthur.'

Again: 'Dearest, Two boys caught it yesterday. We are all in the dumps. Hope you're well. I am sorry not to have been nice to you always.'

And again: 'Dearest, Got a poisoned foot, not serious. Will this war ever turn into peace? Dreamed of you last night, hated waking up. You are too good for me.'

Yet again: 'Dearest, I will not be home for Christmas. Sickening, but cannot desert my men. Probably better off without me. But I aim to mend my ways, given the chance. Best love.'

Jemima wrote back at greater length, ending with coded words of consolation.

'I wish you could be with us at Christmas, but admire your devotion to duty and gallantry ... Wars do end, and we might have many happy years ahead ... The casualties appal us, and I dare not open the front door for fear of a telegram from the War Office ... I live in hopes of beginning again,' she wrote, 'in our very own better world.'

They had never communicated their deeper feelings by word of mouth; but somehow on paper they arrived at the idea that he was doing penance for his evil temper, and that she was offering absolution. He derived some satisfaction from his hardships, and was relieved to fancy that his absence was softening her heart.

The other alleviating factor for Arthur was

his senior NCO, Sergeant Smith, a big strong man, wise and consistently cheerful. The Major and the Sergeant, between them, kept the troops going; and they became friends.

Sergeant Smith had been a builder in Civvy Street, was engaged to a girl who looked pretty in the photograph he showed Arthur, and was not a snob of either kind, neither a social climber nor a class warrior. He repaid the Major's trust in him by reciprocating it. He was in his later twenties, and his nerves withstood the constant stress and the danger.

Arthur was by nature brave, and in fact braver than he seemed, for he felt he was too old for battle; had no stomach for flesh and blood; even his imagination could visualise himself on a stretcher or hooked on the barbed wire of No Man's Land; and he did not want to die before he had merited Jemima's love. He refrained from initiating daredevil schemes, and prayed that he and his soldiers would not be ordered to go over the top and march into German machine-gun fire.

Unfortunately, in his opinion, Sergeant Smith was determined to defeat his country's foes, and tired of dilly-dallying – as he put it – within a stone's throw of the Germans. One day he sought permission to inform his CO that he had been checking the lie of the land and was sure an attack could be mounted on the trenches opposite with minimal risk. How far had he checked, Arthur wished to know. Against orders he had sneaked into No Man's Land at night, Sergeant

Smith confessed. Arthur rebuked him. He wished to hear no more of the matter. But Sergeant Smith supplied further explanations, and revealed that a corporal who was a trained surveyor shared his opinion after studying the terrain. Arthur said that neither Sergeant nor Corporal should have been taking unauthorised action; however, guessing that the information might be common knowledge amongst the soldiery, possibly including officers, he agreed to investigate further.

The upshot was that a raid was planned. Sergeant Smith would lead six men on a detour to a position overlooking the long German trench. They would not have been seen, and would open covering fire on the enemy from the side, enabling a larger body of troops to attack from the front. The risks had been evaluated and were worth taking, and the capture of the opposing trenchwork would be a minor victory for the regiment.

Arthur resigned himself to signalling the start of hostilities at five-thirty as dawn broke on a grey morning. Sergeant Smith began to wriggle his way round on the right, the six other men would follow, and Arthur and his troops were waiting and watching from behind their embankment. There was a distant boom and a shell whistled up, landed with a thump, caused a crater and threw earth into the air. As the earth subsided Sergeant Smith became visible: the hillock that had hidden him was no more, and he was standing up, but clearly wounded and on the point of collapsing. A machine-gun rat-tatted – the Germans were shooting at the wounded man, who reeled under the impact of the bullets.

Arthur roared hoarsely, he was perhaps roaring 'No!' at the machine-gunner, clambered out of the trench, broke through the strands of barbed wire waving his pistol, sprinted across the intervening gap, leapt over the German wire and into the German trench. The machine-gun was silent, pistol shots were heard – the Germans had been laughing at the spectacle of Sergeant Smith, but now Arthur's roars were echoed by other men, and by rifle fire. His junior officers and the troops were following him, gingerly at first, then more enthusiastically as they realised the Germans had left their observation posts to deal with the intruder. A minor massacre was taking place, and continued as the British soldiers reached the edge of the German trench and shot its occupants emerging from dugouts in their nightwear. Arthur had taken everyone by surprise. He had shot the machine-gunner and two other men with his pistol, then invaded a dugout, seized a German rifle and cracked the skulls of the men inside with its butt. With another German rifle he had shot a mound of corpses in pyjamas. He was drenched in blood. He refused furiously to be congratulated. He walked back across No Man's Land, and some soldiers said he was crying.

For his action on that morning he was awarded the Victoria Cross. But he hated talk of his valour and showed it. Jemima read about his medal in the newspapers and wrote to say how proud she and Valentine were. He replied by post: 'The right men never get medals. Mine would have belonged to my Sergeant if there was any justice. I lost my rag again. But that's the last time, I swear.' In 1917 he slipped in the mud of Flanders, broke his pelvis and was invalided home.

The Gorhamburys were pleased to see each other again; but they could not act out the sentiments in their letters, they were too inhibited and inarticulate, and the chasm between his wartime experiences and hers was unbridgeable. He convalesced in his dressing-room, and he never left it. Each of them found the other impossible to touch. He had an accumulation of new concerns, and she was wrapped up in their son.

He gave his Victoria Cross to the girl that Sergeant Smith had hoped to marry.

Jemima was sorry, and said that Valentine would have loved to keep it.

'He'll have too much to keep,' Arthur commented.

'Oh dear!'

'We're too rich.'

'Would you rather be poor?'

He shook his heavy head, not meaning no, rather that it was too difficult a question to answer.

'Arthur, are you happy?'

'What? Of course I am.'

'I hope I haven't done wrong.'

'What? No! That's not it at all. It's the other way round.'

'Can you explain?'

'I'm no good at this sort of talk, Jemima. You mean a lot to me. Can't we leave it at that?'

'Yes – we will – but … The war's over, the past's over. I don't want you to worry.'

'I'm not worrying. I don't know what gave you that idea. Where's Valentine?'

'He's waiting for me upstairs. We're going to catch tadpoles in the pond.'

'Good. Don't let me detain you, my dear.'

'Arthur, thank you for Valentine and everything else. Your son's such a dear boy.'

An Idiot

Arthur, third Marquess, could not agree that Valentine Bushton, in line to be the fourth, was 'dear'. He could see that Valentine meant no harm, but was sure he had a screw loose.

Valentine was seventeen. He looked about fourteen. He was very fair, his complexion and hair verged on albino, he was a throwback to the first Mother Widell, born Ann Dunbee, and he had no beard and was slightly built. Arthur did not hold his son's appearance against him. Arthur was determined to be more than fair to Valentine, to give him the benefit of every doubt, not only on account of paternal feelings, also because he could not forget their potentially lethal row before the war. He was keen to compensate for his violence on that occasion, and reminded himself that Valentine was neither brainless nor charmless, could pass exams, chat to people, please the ladies, ride well and shoot straight. But he suspected that Jemima called their son 'dear' defensively, for the fact of the matter was that Valentine managed to leave a trail of devastation behind him.

He had been obstinate about his Brussels sprouts as a child; but Brussels sprouts were neither the beginning nor the end of his father's disappointment and dissatisfaction. From the earliest age his attitude to property was confused and caused confusion. He gave silver spoons to the servants and got them into trouble. He gave his toys to visiting children, who were smacked for taking them. He presented a gilded clock to a plumber, and an English watercolour to his nanny's sister. At school he reported masters whom he considered unjust to the headmaster, and he refused to abide by the decisions of umpires and referees at games. He was even difficult about the war with the Germans: for a time he claimed to be a pacifist. It was partly because of these scruples of his that Arthur had given away the VC.

When Valentine finished with school, his headmaster's report referred to Lord Bushton's ethical approach to life, and his liberal spirit and praiseworthy intentions. Arthur read it gloomily: he was depressed by the three words which also had negative implications: ethical, liberal and intentions. He was not surprised that Valentine refused to join the army, but ground his teeth when Valentine said he would rather die than go to university, or work in the city, or travel abroad and see the world.

The family solicitors sought a meeting with Lord Bushton before his eighteenth birthday. Mr Higgins and his team had retired, and the new partners were Willmot Willmot and Bagmold. In his own time Valentine sauntered into their premises. Mr Bagmold, a black-haired bespectacled man with a clean-shaven blue chin, greeted his lordship and revealed that he was due to inherit a sizeable sum of money from a Trust Fund set up by an ancestor.

Lord Bushton thanked him without any change of expression.

Mr Bagmold was nonplussed and inquired: 'Shall I say that again, my lord?'

'Not unless you'd like to.'

'No, no – so long as you understand me.'

'I did understand.'

'Have you any questions, my lord?'

'No.'

'May I ask if you'll be celebrating your birthday in style?'

'No – I don't think so,' Valentine replied.

'Oh? Why's that?'

'We don't celebrate birthdays much.'

'I'm sorry to hear it. You'll be stowing your money in the family coffers – very wise!'

'No – you don't understand me – I'll do nothing of the sort – good day, goodbye!'

Valentine qualified this unexpected broadside with one of his mirthless grins. Mr Bagmold ushered his client out with assurances that he had intended no offence.

At Gorhambury Valentine discussed the possibility of a party with his mother.

Jemima wondered why he should want one.

'I don't – not particularly – I was just asking.'

Jemima was against it. She said his father had never gone to a party after giving the one at which he had met her and would not wish to be asked to give another. She mentioned all the work involved and the expense.

'But I'm getting money of my own – I don't want to hoard it or be mean – why shouldn't I spend it as I please?' he objected.

'Oh darling,' Jemima sighed, 'I'd love you to have a party and meet some nice girls, and I'd speak for you if I dared and if it would do any good. But you know your father – he can be awful if he's provoked – and he's old now and in poor health. Please consider postponement. Please – I'm for peace at any price.'

Some weeks elapsed, the birthday was not so far off, and Arthur and Valentine were breakfasting together in the Great Hall.

'Father,' Valentine began.

Arthur looked at him over his newspaper.

'Father, I'll be eighteen soon.'

'What?'

'I've been wondering about a birthday party.'

'Whose birthday?'

'Oh Father – mine – what about a party?'

'Don't be fresh with me, boy!'

'I'm not a boy any more, and I'm thinking of proving how grown up I am by throwing a party on my birthday.'

'Who'll pay? I won't.'

'I don't expect a birthday present from you, Father – you've never given me one.'

'That's cheek.'

'It's the truth.'

'You'll inherit from me – I'll be giving you all I possess – don't you tell me I'm not generous

– you've had the best start in life, and you've got expectations.'

'I know all that, Father, and I thank you.'

'Well – you seem to have forgotten that I could disinherit you.'

'Go ahead – I don't care – I hate money – the last thing I'll ever do is to beg you for money. I only wondered if I could have the party in Gorhambury.'

'Hate money, do you? If you hate it you don't deserve to live in this house, let alone have a party here. Hate money – I'll damn well reconsider my will if you do!'

'Oh Father!'

'Who's paying for your party? Where's the money for that coming from?'

'I'll pay. I can, I'm coming into money on my birthday. Listen, please – I owe people hospitality – it's my turn to be hospitable – and we never invite anyone into this house. I'll throw my party elsewhere if you won't allow me to have it at home.'

'Mind your language! Don't push me!'

'We never talk about anything, Father. We never have. The moment I try to talk you threaten me. I mentioned a birthday party, why does that make you so hot under the collar? I was going to invite you.'

'Don't, don't!'

'Mother's on my side—'

Arthur stood up.

Events followed at literally breakneck speed. Arthur's shoulders were hunched, there was a bull-

173

like hump of muscle at the back of his neck, his head was down and his eyes glared from behind his eyebrows. Valentine also stood, ready to take evasive action but apparently unaware of the impending crisis – he continued to argue his case.

'Mother's on my side, so it's two to one against you, Father.'

Arthur roared: 'I won't be spoken to, I won't be spoken to ...'

'Nor will I be silenced, nor will I be attacked again,' Valentine batted back, as if in a game.

Arthur lumbered towards his son, who nimbly retreated – they were on opposite sides of the long refectory table.

Arthur was roaring and growling as he pursued Valentine round the table.

'Sit down, Father,' Valentine shouted at him. 'You won't catch me – and you wouldn't get a medal if you could – sit down!'

Arthur bellowed and swept all the crockery and silver off the table with a wide sweep of his arm.

'Father!'

Valentine had turned up the volume of his voice. He seemed at last to recognise danger when he saw it. The loudness of his exclamation arrested Arthur, who stopped and froze into immobility. Then all the blood drained from the face of the older man, and he toppled backwards on to the floor. Valentine approached warily. Arthur's arms and legs were twitching and relaxing, and his head bumped backwards on the floorboards.

Harvey, the butler, burst in, and a footman, William. Harvey told Lord Bushton that he could find no pulse in Lord Gorhambury's wrist or his neck. Valentine sent for his mother. When she entered the Great Hall in a rush, her hair disarrayed and wearing a negligée, he grinned at her and said: 'Father's dead.'

Naturally Jemima was shocked by the sudden death of her husband. She was more so by the grin of her son when he announced it.

What had he meant? His grin was nothing to do with humour. It might be an admission that he had made a mistake. It expressed bafflement and perhaps despair. The meaning it forced her to recognise was that he was far from normal.

Yet Valentine helped to organise his father's funeral, and played his part in the service with dignity. On the other hand he was still set on having a big birthday bash a month afterwards. His mother, local dignitaries and even his few young friends pointed out that a party would look like a celebration of his translation into a marquess and his haul of golden etceteras: he shook his head and ordered the invitation cards. Jemima had to din it into him that she would not and he should not dance on the unsettled grave of her spouse, his benefactor, and a national hero.

She then had to bring Valentine round to acceptance of an interval, a pause before he shouldered the burdens of his inheritance. She took him to inspect an educational establishment in Switzerland: he was excited by the snow. He met the Principal, who returned his grin with a straightforward smile. He enrolled for a three year course; and subsided as he had in his years at English schools, and as Jemima had ventured to hope.

Aged nearly twenty-one he was taller and stronger, good-looking in his pale blond way, and gently agreeable and even charming.

He revived his plan for a birthday party. It would be his real coming-of-age ball. This time no one objected. Again the invitations were printed – and sent out.

On the night of the ball the great house was floodlit, and its myriad windows emitted light. The food and the wines were prepared, a band played, and the Marquess and his mother greeted their guests, the women in more or less restraining gowns and jewellery, the girls in their eye-catching finery, and the men in stiff shirts, white ties and tails.

Valentine inaugurated the proceedings by dancing with Jemima. They both looked happy, and the dark chapter of family history, the late Marquess's unaccountable death, and the rumours and gossip that had circulated about his son, seemed to have given way to a propitious new beginning.

Valentine was still a virgin. He had been a late developer, and in Switzerland there were skiing and skating in winter and tennis and long walks in summer. He had never been troubled by the lusts of the flesh: his constitution was generally low-toned. Besides, he was prim and had principles. But at the ball he was at last stirred by the enthusiastic greetings of local girls with whom he had played at children's parties, and by the attentions of unknown women of all ages, invited by his mother.

He danced with one girl after another. He circled round in the Paul Joneses and danced with whichever girl was in front of him when the music stopped. Some of his partners were anonymous, but one impressed him by not being alarmingly pretty, by her friendliness and easy laughter. She was called Lucy Haverlock. He met her in a Paul Jones, then picked her out to dance with him three more times. She was tall, heavily built, had brown hair and rather small bright brown eyes. She laughed at his little jokes and her high spirits were infectious. He was sorry when she said she had to leave.

It was late or early – a lot of guests were leaving and bidding him goodbye, good night or good morning. Lucy Haverlock was in the queue and introduced him to her mother, Lady Haverlock, who invited him to stay for a weekend at the Haverlock home in Dorset.

Valentine and Lucy met again by chance at entertainments in London – he was invited to them by people who had been at the Gorhambury ball. He was relieved to recognise a friend amongst all the strangers and walked with her at the Zoo party, sat with her at the theatre party, and danced with her a few times at the party in a house in Park Lane. They got on pretty well together. He was not a great talker, but he could smile as well as grin, he had a sweet innocent smile, and he smiled at her chatter and answered her questions. Their fourth meeting was at a ball in a suburban house with a large garden. By then Valentine was more in demand as a dancing partner, although his uncertain steps on the dance-floor might not have been his main attraction, and he only asked Lucy to dance once. Afterwards she clung on to him – figuratively – by suggesting that they should stroll in the garden illuminated by Chinese lanterns.

He agreed. They walked away from the music and lights. She took his hand in hers, and the night closed in around them.

She said to him, 'Valentine, I do like you,' and he said, 'Well, I like you.'

Silence fell.

She asked: 'Are you wanting to be back at the ball?'

'That's an idea,' he replied.

'Oh!' she commented in a new tone of voice, a sulky tone, let go of his hand, turned as if with a toss of her head, and marched ahead of him towards the house.

Before they reached the first or last lantern she stopped and said: 'Thanks for the dance,' and kissed him on his cheek and somehow on his lips.

'Good night – until the weekend,' she said, and laughed and rejoined the throng in the ballroom.

On the Friday afternoon of his visit he drove to Haverlock Manor in his Rover, arriving in time for tea. He was greeted by Lucy and by her mother, and had his hand shaken hard by Sir Austin, a small bustling person, recently knighted for his services in the City of London and for philanthropical work in his county. Valentine was apparently the sole guest. Lucy's parents were more respectful than he wished them to be, and he squirmed when Sir Austin requested permission to call him by his Christian name.

After tea Lucy took him for a walk. In effect it was more a talk than a walk. She said her father was bossy and her mother a silly fool, and that she intended not to hang about at home for much longer. She yearned for a house of her own and to be happy there with her children. She criticised her girlfriends for being frivolous and flirty, and said that 'underneath' she was 'serious'. She aired her views to which he responded with vague encouragement, and they both lost track of time. They had to retrace their steps in a hurry to change clothes and be ready for dinner.

Sir Austin did the talking during the meal. He boasted about his wines and his daughter; his connections with important people Valentine had never heard of; his charity work with unmarried mothers and criminals; and the bricks and mortar, formerly known as The Grange, that he had renamed Haverlock Manor, although it was stockbrokers' Tudor and in no sense manorial.

Lucy removed Valentine as soon as she could to the room where she had been taught her ABC, the so-called schoolroom, a word with a double meaning in present circumstances. She wound up the gramophone and they danced. She danced closer and closer and soon cheek to cheek, and not long afterwards they were kissing. Her kisses became educational, and Valentine was stimulated to an embarrassing degree. At some point she opened a window and they leant out: it was like coming up for air.

Then Sir Austin arrived with Lady Haverlock in his wake and said it was bedtime. Lucy frowned at her parents behind their backs and shook her head and smirked at Valentine, who grinned in response. At the top of the stairs they all said good night and Valentine shut the door of his bedroom.

The next day, Saturday, was quite 'okay', as he described it to himself. He played tennis with Lucy in the morning and early afternoon, and was shown off to neighbours who came to tea. At dinner Sir Austin sampled his wines to such an extent that he spent the rest of the evening trying to prove that Valentine's family history was not more noteworthy than his own.

Later on, Valentine, alone in his bedroom, was not altogether sorry to have dodged his lessons in the schoolroom. His naivety notwithstanding, he sensed that kissing and being kissed by Lucy could be leading in a dangerous direction.

On the Sunday morning after breakfast Sir Austin suggested a chinwag in his business room, where he sat one side of his mammoth desk and Valentine on the other.

He began: 'I wish to talk to you about your friendship with my daughter. Lucy's particularly fond of you, and I believe and hope that you reciprocate. Nothing would please me more than your and her agreement to make a match of it, but my wife and I would not dream of interfering or putting pressure on either party. The decision is yours. However, I feel it's right and proper to mention that Lucy has considerable expectations. You're a wealthy man, but I am by no means a poor one, and she's my only child and her husband will have many reasons of the most practical sort to be grateful to her.'

'Do you mean money?'

'And property.'

'No – I'm not interested – thank you.'

'Excuse me?'

'I don't like money.'

'My dear boy, you're thinking it's love that makes the world go round, you still have to learn that it's filthy lucre.'

'I don't hold with that.'

'Please mind your manners, Valentine.'

'Sorry – it's all a muddle – you're so wide of the mark!'

'And I'm sorry your father's not still alive. He was a great man and would knock sense into your head.'

'He tried to, he knocked me out when I was young, but I had my own back.'

'What are you saying?'

'I killed my father.'

'What?'

'It doesn't matter.'

'What have you said? What did you do?'

'I killed my father by accident. It's beside the point. I can't marry Lucy. She's very nice, but I never meant to marry her, sorry!'

'This is most disturbing.'

'I'd better leave your house.'

'You must have misled Lucy.'

'Not on purpose. We ... Thank you for your kindness. Goodbye.'

Both men stood up.

Sir Austin said: 'You'll have to tell Lucy.'

Valentine said: 'Will I?' – and grinned.

Sir Austin stared at him, went redder in the face, and shouted: 'Get out, go!'

Valentine retreated.

Lucy had been waiting in the hall and had heard her father's raised voice.

She rushed at Valentine, asking, 'What's happened?'

He replied: 'Sorry – all a mistake – oh dear – I'm off.'

He ran towards the stairs, heading for his bedroom and his luggage – she pursued him with questions.

He answered her while he opened his suitcase and packed his things.

'Your father was wrong ... It's my fault, not his ... You've all been so kind ... I do like you, Lucy, but better all round if I leave you in peace.'

She did not take it well. She flushed and

frowned. She said nothing was funny, referring to his grins. She swore that she hated him. She retired hurt, sobbing and slamming the door.

He crept down the back stairs with his suitcase and drove his Rover back to Gorhambury.

His mother asked him if he had enjoyed his weekend with the Haverlocks.

He grinned by way of answer.

Jemima therefore feared it had been a disaster, and commented as if to show solidarity with him whatever he had done: 'Vera Haverlock's a nice woman, but her husband's pushy and that daughter of theirs looks alarming.'

Valentine changed the subject.

He continued to live with his mother, and months and then years passed. There was another long lull in the storminess of his biography. He divided his time between a little work at Gorhambury and more play in London and elsewhere. Sometimes he invited friends to stay, couples, elderly ladies, bachelors, never an unattached young woman: which reinforced Jemima's suspicion that he had been frightened by Lucy Haverlock.

She and Valentine cohabited without friction, although she was completely nonplussed by him, and aware that it was also the other way round. He seemed not to know anybody well, nor to need to do so, yet his detachment from mundane matters, his unworldliness combined with benevolence, had attractions. She smiled at his crazes –

turning part of the Forest of Woody into an arboretum open to the public, building rows of alms houses – and took care not to criticise. She was sorry about his apparent lack of interest in the opposite sex, and hoped it was temporary or that he had a mistress somewhere; but she was in no hurry for him to marry and evict her from her comfortable home.

He himself might have meant to hide at Gorhambury after his flight from Haverlock Manor. He might have had a fancy to do penance for the accumulation of his errors, failures, trespasses and sins. But a marquess and a magnate, youthful and personable, is never allowed to seek premature interment in the wilderness. He was winkled out by the Establishment. He could not refuse to be a Deputy Lord Lieutenant of his county and a Justice of the Peace. He was summoned to vote in the House of Lords. He had to grant coach parties access to his house on certain days. And he had an estate, a land agent, tenants, employees, solicitors, stockbrokers and a bank: a sentence figured in his nightmares, 'May I have a word with you, my lord?'

It was the mid-thirties. The politicians were brewing another world war, and internationally the pace of fun grew hectic. Valentine was an exception to the rule of eat, drink, be merry and kiss-me-quick; but he was pliant and compliant. He accepted invitations because to refuse them was often more troublesome: he did not want to be asked for a different date, or be cast in the role of wet blanket. He grinned and bore his lot. People sent him snapshots of himself in Scotland, St Moritz, Paris, New York, Hollywood and Hong Kong. In one he is shooting, in others playing croquet; dressed up as a woman for charades; having lunch *al fresco* with the Fairbanks; sunbathing on the Duke of Westminster's yacht. Girls are never far away from him photographically: they link their arms in his, blow kisses at him, pour libations into glasses he holds out, carry his cartridge case, even sit on his knee.

He was prepared to be their pet. He was the personification of nothing doing. He preferred to amuse women with his lack of a recognisable sense of humour. He did not care if his chastity was mistaken for disablement: he had dared to purchase introductions to angels of the night.

The news that Lucy Haverlock was engaged to marry an Argentinian polo-player had a slightly liberating effect on Valentine; but age had not made him more romantic, quite the opposite, and the idea of his procreational obligations had not yet crossed his mind.

As he moved in the highest social circles and the smartest of sets, it was a foregone conclusion that he would make the acquaintance of the Prince of Wales of the day, son of King George V and great-grandson of Queen Victoria, who had created his marquessate. They met in a nightclub. The Prince was a very small fair-haired man, who cleared his throat before speaking and was inclined to laugh at weak jokes. Valentine was soon on a list of persons fit to be invited

185

to princely entertainments and to be a fellow guest of HRH. He repeatedly shook the royal hand, but never exchanged more than greetings and platitudes – there were always too many people, courtiers and riff-raff, pressing in. Some months after the death of King George V, he was invited by the former Prince of Wales, now King Edward VIII awaiting coronation, to spend a long weekend and shoot at Sandringham in Norfolk. The house party of about twenty people was interesting in that it included Mrs Simpson, the black-haired angular American woman who was rumoured to be, and hoisted signals that she was, the mistress of the new king.

His Majesty soon discovered that Valentine's family name had originally been Widdle, and laughed and caused others to laugh about it for three and a half days.

Mrs Simpson tried to console him for being the butt of such jocularity thus: 'I'd rather be a Widdle than the other thing you English people call me' – which he thought unladylike.

Not long after that weekend King Edward abdicated.

Valentine was astounded. He even winced at the soupy excuses the former king advanced for rejecting a throne, an empire, and betraying the worldwide millions of his loyal subjects. He was not so unworldly as to fail to marvel at the worst bargain ever struck in the whole of history – everything, every material thing that human destiny could offer and spiritual things to boot, for next to nothing.

It startled him. He was reminded of the duty he himself had not discharged to sire a son and heir. But he had never been much good at concentrating, and was now diverted from his reproductive intention by the call to arms. War seemed inevitable, and, as honorary colonel-in-chief of his county regiment, he felt honour bound to train with his troops and qualify to lead them into battle. The possibility that he might fall on the battlefield, indeed the likelihood considering his clumsiness, reinforced the message that he ought to breed before it was too late. Typically, he procrastinated. He could foresee unpleasantness between his mother and his wife.

His final push in a matrimonial direction was Jemima's death from pneumonia in the spring of 1939. He had not wished for it; but it was so convenient that he grinned when Dr Harbert, the family's general practitioner, broke the tragic news.

During a couple of months of mourning he selected Rosemary Staple-Miller for participation in his project. He ran into her at a charity bash, invited her to tea at Gorhambury and showed her round the house. Her tongue-tied embarrassment impressed him favourably. He asked her to lunch and conducted a tour of his estate. He then spoke to her father, Bobby Staple-Miller, an estate agent, who bowed and scraped to signify that he was all for the union.

Rosemary was young, and presumably virginal, a buxom little blonde, curly-headed and blue-eyed. Her father was popular in Gorham and her mother, Greta, was in charge of the Women's Institute and the Girl Guides. Valentine was sure she would do. She almost fainted when he proposed to her. He supported her and said that he knew he was too old for her and he would not take it amiss if she turned him down. But she must have thought his arm round her shoulders was an embrace, for she revived and kissed him forcefully, repeating the two words: 'Why me?'

Valentine grinned a bit, but she was perhaps too excited to notice, and was not discouraged.

There was no premarital dalliance. For three months they met only at social celebrations or to plan the wedding with her mother and others. At least and at last their marriage was consummated in Paris. The honey seeped out of their honeymoon nonetheless. He bought more newspapers and she spent more time in the shops. One day she called him 'lovey' and he corrected her. On another he talked to her about the risk of war and she corrected him: 'I'm not interested in things like that.' But three persons returned from where two had gone, and pregnancy turned failure into partial success.

Back at Gorhambury, he resumed his work in the Estate Office, and she busied herself with household affairs. They put in appearances together at social gatherings, otherwise did not see a lot of each other, and in view of her pregnancy he slept in his dressing-room.

War was duly declared in September, and Valentine warned Rosemary that he would be joining the army in the near future.

After dinner on the day he issued his warning she spoke to him on an unusually serious subject. She asked for money. She said Gorhambury was grim, she wanted to brighten it up, paint everything, make structural changes, and she would love to have a free hand to improve the garden.

Valentine grew restless.

Rosemary noted his restlessness and became more insistent: 'I haven't got any money, and nothing's settled as it should have been. What am I expected to do? When are you going to help me and take care of your child?'

'I pay for everything,' he said.

'But now you're leaving us penniless – and horrid things happen in a war – it isn't right, Valentine – can't you understand?'

'Stop, stop!' he cried out, covering his ears with his hands. 'Go to bed, Rosemary. Go, please!'

She obeyed him. She was frightened. He too was frightened in case he would prove to be his father's son and lose control of himself. But the next day he had cooled down sufficiently to call on Mr Bagmold, who was now the head of the firm of his family's solicitors. He explained abruptly why he was sitting in Mr Bagmold's office: no marriage settlement on his wife and no will, and he was about to go on active service.

Blue-chinned Mr Bagmold mentioned the letters he had written to Lord Gorhambury, begging him to deal with such matters.

'Sorry – I don't read my letters often – better do everything here and at once.'

'Yes, my lord. What sum of money would you wish to settle on her ladyship?'

'I don't know. She's not used to money. Ten thousand for herself, ten thousand for redecorating the house – what do you think?'

'And in your will, my lord?'

'Double – twenty thousand for herself, another twenty for exceptional payments – and all the money in a trust fund, so that she won't spend it too quickly.'

'The rest of your fortune to be left to your child whether male or female?'

'There's no one else to inherit it – I've no male relations, I've lost touch with my female cousins – anyway my father said he had surrendered the right of Widell women to bear the title. Can I leave it to you to draw up the papers?'

'Who is to have the power of attorney while you serve in the army, my lord?'

'God knows! You'll have to look after things. The war could well mean ruination – there might not be a fortune to worry about.'

'I sincerely hope that will not be the case, Lord Gorhambury.'

'Do you? I don't. Have I given you enough information to draw up the necessary papers?'

'My lord, before we go further I should advise you that her ladyship has already spoken to me regarding these issues.'

'How's that?'

'She came here with her parents. I have been friendly with the Staple-Miller family since I was a child.'

'But they spoke to you on business?'

'Yes, sir.'

'What did they want?'

'More than you think of giving Lady Gorhambury, if I may put it that way.'

'How much more?'

'Your father-in-law, Bobby Staple-Miller, has a professional eye for the value of property. The Staple-Miller family on the whole are counting on your figures multiplied by twenty, roughly speaking – a settlement of two hundred thousand, four hundred thousand if the money for interior decoration is included, and getting on for a million via your will.'

Valentine grinned.

'She didn't tell me.'

'I apologise for worrying your lordship.'

'You were right. You weren't wrong.'

'How am I to proceed?'

'Do as she wishes. How soon will the papers be ready for me to sign?'

'I could draft something for you to sign, if you agreed with the contents, in two days. But I'm not sure of your wishes, not precisely, my lord.'

'My wishes are to be rid of it all, the paperwork and the money. Make your power of attorney valid from today.'

Mr Bagmold hummed and hawed, but Valentine cut him short and left the premises.

The two days elapsed. Rosemary had been having breakfast in bed on doctor's orders. At ten in the morning Valentine entered her bedroom in the military uniform complete with Sam Browne belt of a second lieutenant.

She screamed. He explained that he was on his way to report to the barracks of his regiment, and had been told that he and other men would be joining the British Expeditionary Force in France with minimum delay.

'Oh Valentine,' she exclaimed, but with a hint of query in her voice.

He said: 'I shall be signing the papers that affect you.'

'Oh Valentine,' she repeated, gratefully but still with a query in her voice.

'You're getting what you and your parents put in for. I know you tackled Bagmold behind my back.'

'I didn't, we didn't, we only asked advice – I haven't done anything naughty, don't scold me today of all days. Thank you, Valentine – I'll try my best to give you a son. Please kiss me goodbye – and come home safely.'

He obliged with a kiss and grinned at her from the doorway.

Rupert Robert Widell, Lord Bushton, was born three months later. Valentine received the news through regimental channels. Then a note from Rosemary reached him: Rupert was a lovely little boy, he and she were both well. She had her money and was thrilled with it, and she hoped Valentine was all right.

On the day her note arrived he and the rest

of the British army began their retreat from France. He lost his bearings as he led his platoon towards the French coast. A road they were on was blocked by a burned-out British tank, in front of which was a sign with the word Dunkirk scrawled on it and an arrow pointing to a lane. He and his men were pleased to believe that they had an outside chance of rescue – they had heard of boats sailing across from England to save soldiers on the Dunkirk beaches. They drove along the lane and straight into a makeshift camp for Germany's prisoners of war.

Valentine's war ended there. He had not won a VC of his own, was awarded no medal for gallantry, or any commendation for his inglorious conduct in action. On the other hand, imprisonment suited him. He had virtually nothing to do. He offended no one, had no pretensions, was neither stand-offish nor bossy, and public opinion in the camp was that he could almost be forgiven for being a marquess. Of course he differed from the other prisoners, but not only because of his class. He was not frustrated, was relieved to be out of range of women, and glad that his wife's letters had to be short and he had excuses for not always answering them.

Rosemary's first letter began to tell the story of their marriage during the war.

'Darling Valentine, Rupert's doing well, and I hope you are. But we are going to have evacuees from the East End of London at Gorhambury. They are already in the cottages by the kennels and some are in the stables. I know they and their children are safer here than they would be in town, but they are absolute rag-tag-and-bobtails, they really are, and I don't see why they have to be on our doorstep. Nigel Bagmold said you instructed him to let them in. Can this be true? Please do stop it happening.'

Her next included the following: 'Not a word from you, and Nigel tells me he has heard nothing. I hope it doesn't mean you're ill. Anway, the situation here is going from bad to worse. We now have fourteen mothers with their grubby children parked on this place. I can scarcely be sorry for them, or polite. Nigel won't stop it, and says you wanted evacuees in the Bachelor Wing – you wouldn't want them if you had to live in a slum.'

Again: 'Valentine, there are twenty-six strangers in what was your home and in Rupert's and mine. They're in the Bachelor Wing, but the children stray – I found two in my bathroom the other day, and their mothers' apologies are not good enough. It's cruel of you to have visited all this on a wife who's been missing her husband for nearly a year. Why do you refuse to face up to the issue in your letters? I haven't heard a word of explanation or sympathy.'

Yet again: 'I'm convinced you gave orders to Nigel to house these evacuees to punish me for having asked you to treat me properly and indeed legally in a financial sense. It wasn't kind of you, Valentine – I'm suffering because of your unkindness, and so is your son who is picking up cockney words and pronunciations. I did not go behind your back, I merely called on an old friend of myself and my parents, I committed no crime but you're punishing me all the same. My father thinks it's ungentlemanly.'

However, towards the end of the second year of Valentine's imprisonment, Rosemary wrote: 'Nigel says that no more evacuees can be fitted in, which is a relief, and he thinks the end of the war may be in sight and that they will then go back to London. I hope he's not too optimistic, although I must say his optimism has been the greatest help to me. He has also tried to provide the explanation that I have not received from you. He calls you an idealist who would like to compensate for your birth and breeding and great inheritance. That's all fine and dandy, as our American allies would say, but please never forget Rupert, who might grow up to have very different ideas and should not be denied his birthright. Nigel sends his regards.'

A letter from Nigel Bagmold himself filled a gap in the correspondence.

After a polite sentence or two he wrote: 'I regret to inform you that I have entrusted your papers and power of attorney to my colleague Graeme Hose, who is now the senior partner of this firm and a first-class lawyer. I am moving to London to set up a legal consultancy and shall live in the pleasant suburb of Dulwich. I would like to thank you yet again for trusting me to attend to the management of the Gorhambury Estate. Although you wished me not to bother you with reports, I believe you would wish to know that evacuees now inhabit the thirty-two habitations that were and have been made habitable.'

In the fourth year of the war Valentine received a letter from Mr Hose of Hose and Drewett, rendering accounts of their stewardship of the estate and ending with another reference to the evacuees.

'Many would now like to return to London, but they have no home to go to and no money to purchase accommodation there. They repeatedly say how lucky they have been to find shelter at Gorhambury. The sad fact remains that families who stayed put in London and survived may have been luckier.'

Shortly before the Germans surrendered Rosemary wrote a last letter to Valentine.

'I'm sorry if this letter spoils your homecoming, but perhaps it will have the opposite effect. I must ask you for a divorce. It was good of you to marry me, and I hope you will be good and let me go. We were never right for each other. But without the war, and you being miles away in prison and me being so lonely and miserable, who knows? The extraordinary thing was that somebody fell in love with me, and I with him, while you were gone. He is a very good man, too. He's Nigel Bagmold. I spent a lot of time in his house in Dulwich after Gorhambury became uninhabitable, although Rupert remained in your home and with his Nanny Jones throughout. I am with Nigel now. He sends you his compliments. We will not be at Gorhambury to greet or embarrass you on your return. Rupert is looking forward to knowing his father.'

Valentine did not write to Rosemary again. He was not well, he had not been well for months, his health had not withstood the hardships of prison and the North German winters. He was not surprised by his wife's letter, although he grinned when he read the name of Nigel Bagmold in the space reserved for her lover.

Release and repatriation occurred, and at last he limped into Gorhambury, thin and wan, and met Rupert, Nanny, and Ida and Daisy, the two daily ladies who had cooked and cleaned for his family for the duration.

The next day he telephoned Mr Hose. He spoke about money, was pleased to learn there was still a lot left, and said he wanted to spend it all in a certain way. Mr Hose asked if he could bring Mr Drewett with him to Gorhambury in order to discuss his lordship's intentions. Valentine agreed; and duly explained again, or insisted, that houses in the East End of London damaged or destroyed by enemy action were to be bought at pre-war prices, rebuilt, refurbished, and either let at peppercorn rents to evacuees or sold to those who wished to borrow money from himself at advantageous rates. Mr Hose was horrified, and Mr Drewett said it was nothing like business. Valentine replied that he was determined to help people, especially the poor ones who were homeless because of the war. The solicitors argued that he should not deplete the resources of his family by somewhat illogical generosity carried to extremes. He silenced them by suggesting that he might charge their former colleague, Bagmold, with carrying out his scheme, if they found it so objectionable.

Valentine divested himself of his money with satisfaction. Mr Hose reported that it was running out: his lordship issued orders to sell the Forest of Woody and Goatacre Farm. Queues formed outside the offices of Hose and Drewett in Gorham. Public opinion was divided: Lord Gorhambury had either been driven over the edge by Hitler, his wife, Nigel Bagmold, and his bad-tempered father, or was a saint. He refused to listen to pleas submitted on behalf of his heir, and to advice that he needed psychological as well as medical assistance.

He dozed in his study. He let his grey beard grow. He and Rupert met on some strange common ground of fantasies that nobody else could understand – they whispered and giggled together. When only the house, its contents, the park, and a small capital sum remained for Rupert to inherit, Valentine called a halt to his financial dealings.

He divorced Rosemary without seeing her again. He let Rupert go to stay with her in Dulwich. At an inconvenient moment he had to authorise his solicitors to ask his ex-wife to forgo certain quarterly dues from the Gorhambury Estate. She agreed; but she also wrote to him to say what a shame it was that he was such an idiot.

He did not mind much. He was as sure of

himself as idiots often are. He surrendered to the doctors who wanted to treat his tuberculosis. He spent the next three years in various hospitals and sanitaria.

He was still an invalid when he was allowed back to Gorhambury and to see his son. One day he had to sanction the sale of a row of the houses in London he had bought. There were ten of them, in a terrace, all bomb-damaged, not built up, freehold but uninhabitable. He had paid five thousand for the lot. They were sold for fifty thousand. He had innumerable other houses bought at roughly the same price, many still empty, many let to tenants. Their value had already appreciated by a thousand per cent, and Mr Hose was happy to predict that they would be worth ten times more in next to no time. Valentine, whose motives had been philanthropic, who had tried to strip his family of excessive wealth, realised with a first and last ache of disappointment in himself that he had made it richer than it ever had been.

Nanny Jones, bringing Rupert downstairs to play with his father, found him lying on the floor of his study.

Blessings in Disguise

The Marchioness of Gorhambury, ex-wife of the late Marquess, mother of his son, the eleven-year-old Marquess, and wife of Nigel Bagmold whose name she refused to take, Rosemary Staple-Miller of yore, considered it right and proper for her boy Rupert to move out of the Bagmold residence, Tall Pines, Dulwich, London S.E., and into his family seat. Considering his tender years, and his parents' divorce and the loss of his father, his mother also moved back into Gorhambury to care for poor Rupert, and Bagmold came too.

Rosemary was conventional. She therefore wore black for Valentine and the diamond bracelet he had given her and her two wedding rings, and managed to look sad for the usual period of mourning. After the funeral she also forced her Rupert and her Nigel to wear black armbands.

The residential upheaval was exciting. Nigel Bagmold's blue chin had shone when she proposed it and he had said: 'I feel sure your former husband would wish us to settle his heir into the little chap's rightful home. I can travel up from Gorham to Dulwich to attend to my legal commitments in London.' Rosemary thanked her husband for his unselfishness, and Rupert conveyed the impression that he belonged in a house, a big one, rather than in a cramped villa in the suburbs of London.

Rosemary had had her cake and was eating it. She had married miles above her, and believed herself to be a real life Cinderella. But her princely Marquess had disappointed her in most ways, condemned her to live with vulgar evacuees in the war, and after the war refused to see her. On the other hand she had stumbled into the arms of a virile lawyer who had guided her through her divorce, married her and been pleased to be a Marchioness's plain mister. And now she would again rule the roost in the marble halls and state apartments of Gorhambury. She was aware of being envied, and she gloried in it.

She gloried temporarily. For one thing, she had to live in a sort of building site while the room-dividers and the conduits for water, gas and electricity installed for evacuees were removed, and the rooms were made good and repainted. For another more important thing, her difficulties with Rupert intensified – they seemed to increase in line with his discovery of the size of his inheritance. Yes, true, she had everything, but the everything she had was a Pandora's Box from which a contrary and alarming creature was emerging; and, worst luck, she was barren and could not dilute his upsetting influence by bearing some straightforward Bagmolds.

Rupert had been the prettiest baby to look at but painful to breast-feed – and so their relationship developed. She doted on him and he tortured her in one way or another. He was bright and all too clever for her. He was delightful, a treasure, but had no appetite and over-reacted to minor ailments. He was disobedient and apparently felt bound to break every rule. He pleased and he provoked her, he was sweet and he was spiteful. He tied her in knots, eluded and exasperated her, yet won her at will with his platinum-blond curls and pale blue eyes that watched unblinkingly. He not only gained control over her, but also persuaded her that she was not worthy of him, was clumsy and stupid and ugly and a failure in all respects.

There was hostility between Rupert and Nigel, and she could not bring about peace or an armistice. Rupert was apt to call Nigel 'Mouldy'. When Nigel reasoned with him, Rupert yodelled 'Bla bla bla!' When Rosemary asked Rupert what was wrong with his stepfather, she was told: 'He's a solicitor – Father was a marquess.' Rosemary had allowed Rupert to make up his face with her cosmetics, Nigel forbad it, and a row ensued. Nigel would not let Rupert swap clothing with the girls at kindergarten – another row. Nigel sided with the headmaster of Rupert's preparatory school, who said Rupert was a mischiefmaker – more rows.

Later on, Rupert's housemaster at his public school, to which he was despatched by his mother and stepfather for three blessedly long terms of boarding annually, wrote worrying reports: 'Lord Gorhambury is rather too conscious of his social position ... is not interested in school work and thinks himself sophisticated ... is a disruptive influence – supercilious – flirtatious – not ready for confirmation – not a player of boys' games ... could be in danger of the sack if he does not pull his socks up.'

Nigel was prevailed upon to ask for an explanation of some of these comments.

'I hope you're not a snob, Rupert,' he said.

'Not as much as you are,' Rupert retorted.

Nigel tried again.

'What does flirtatious mean, who do you flirt with, and why are you in danger of the sack?'

'You know what sodomites are, don't you, Nigel?'

'Pardon? I'm sorry to hear you speak that word. My answer's irrelevant. But what is yours? I hope you're not engaged in unnatural practices.'

'Nobody bullies me.'

'Is that your answer?'

'Wouldn't you like to know!'

At least Rupert was not sacked, and Nigel assured Rosemary that his head was in the clouds and the same probably applied to his body.

His holidays at Gorhambury were no easier to understand than his terms at school. He scribbled in his bedroom on sunny summer days. He spent hours in his room, decorating it with paper cutouts and home-made streamers. He picked flowers for his room and refused to allow his mother into it. He went missing at mealtimes; and when he did present himself was either stubbornly silent or would launch into a dissertation on the boy-poets he hoped to emulate, Chatterton and Rimbaud, who respectively committed suicide and might have become a slave driver in Africa.

Aged fourteen he took his mother to task about her title.

'You're not a Lady, mother,' he remarked.

She took it the wrong way and accused him of insulting her.

'You're really Mrs Bagmold,' he explained.

But she took that the wrong way too, and began to whimper.

'Oh Mother,' he scolded, 'why do you want to be a marchioness when you're not one?'

'It's the title your father gave me, and I'd hate to cast it off like an old shoe.'

'You cast Father off like an old shoe.'

'I didn't – it was the other way round – he joined the army and went to the war without saying goodbye properly – and he plagued me with his evacuees and made a muddle and a mess of Gorhambury. And now you're being cruel and horrid. I'm not horrid to you, although you're as contrary as you can be. I believe in live and let live.'

'You believe in making me live with somebody who's using the name that only belongs to the woman I marry.'

'What are you saying? What do you mean?'

'You're pretending you're still Father's wife. But you married a second husband, and Father's dead, and you're not entitled to pose as his widow.'

'Oh that's so unkind! You don't know how unkind you're being, Rupert – one day I'll explain why I finished with your father. You're too young to understand. Please stop!'

'Well, I shall tell people you're Mrs Bagmold.'

'Nigel will be cross with you if you do – Nigel's going to be furious with you for treating me like this.'

'He should be proud to have a missis instead of another man's marchioness.'

The conclusion of this argument was predictable. Rupert came out on top because he was logical and ruthless, also because he was beginning to appreciate his power and acquiring a taste for exercising it.

Four years passed. Gorhambury was not a happy house in Rupert's holidays from school. He created disharmony. He was argumentative and opinionated. He pursued his outlandish hobbies – creating a grotto with seashells, for example – and invited his schoolfriends to stay, youths who giggled when Rosemary asked if they were keen on hunting, shooting or fishing. Mother and stepfather felt under threat, as if they were cohabiting with the representative of another species, who seemed to have cannibalistic tendencies. The differences of opinion, the clashes and quarrels culminated in history repeating itself: that is, in discussion of plans to celebrate the eighteenth birthday of his lordship.

Rupert was set on a ball, but a ball different from and more magnificent than the balls given by his forebears, for a thousand guests, with dancing in the streets for the people of Gorham, and fountains in the market place spouting French wine. He wanted to eradicate memories of evacuees, bombs and bereavement. Rosemary was alarmed. She had heard that the local nickname for Rupert was 'gormless', because he looked so feeble and foolish: she referred to the advantages of keeping a low profile. She was apprehensive that her son and she herself would be criticised for frittering away the Widell wealth which the late Marquess had tried, mercifully in vain, to devote to the poor. When she stammered and was snubbed by Rupert, Nigel voiced objections. He stroked his blue chin and asked rhetorically: was it a good idea to flaunt opulence in an increasingly egalitarian world? He estimated the cost of Rupert's flamboyant fancy, and warned of the extent of capital outlay and loss of income.

The argument ground on for several days. One evening at dinner, as three were proving not to be good company, Nigel and Rosemary urged a compromise, festivities more glamorous than they had envisaged and less prodigal than Rupert had hoped for.

The latter pondered it, head lowered and eyes down. His fair hair was shoulder-length, his forehead and complexion white and possibly powdered, his features fine if bony, and his jaw contradictory, muscular and jutting. He wore a jacket he had designed, a 'smoking jacket', made of brown velvet and edged with gold braid.

He looked up, all blue eyes and white eyelashes,

and said to his mother and stepfather: 'I've a better idea. You two clear out of Gorhambury – chop chop, at once.'

Rupert postponed his party: it might never have been more than a tease. He did have words with Messrs Hose and Drewett, the former in heavy horn-rims and the latter in rimless spectacles. They told him the family finances were in better shape than for many years, owing to his father's well-timed purchase of London property and his own lengthy minority and consequential savings. Some London houses had been disposed of, registering welcome capital gains, but a few more would have to be sold to raise money to complete the refurbishment of Gorhambury and to pay for the repurchase of the Forest of Woody and Goatacre Farm. Certain family portraits were also about to be bought back by the Gorhambury Estate. In other words, words that were not quite spoken, sanity had prevailed over the radical plans and waywardness of the late Marquess. But the solicitors, who thought they had saved the day for common sense and the Widell family, cleared their throats when Rupert mentioned the ball, and could only summon cautious smiles when he said he would not be giving it just yet.

He opted for foreign travel. He would do a tour that would be grander than the old Grand Tour until his estate was again in full working order.

Four years after he had left Gorhambury, four years and a few months since he had evicted the Bagmolds, as he chose to call them, he returned with friends, a dozen or so. More friends arrived and none seemed to depart. It was soon known that the house was not great enough to hold so many young people, and the servants told tales of sleeping-bags and futons, of dormitories, staggered meals, high jinks and goings-on. The natives of Gorham were startled to see these Bohemians, gypsies, new-age-travellers, flower children, junkies, crackpots or whatever they were, wandering the streets in groups, browsing in the chemists' shops, and buying suspect herbs, artists' materials and the sauciest postcards.

Their host, the Marquess, was occasionally seen in public places, though he refused formal engagements and invitations. He looked less of a stripling, not quite so gormless. But his garb was alien, sarongs and kaftans, bandannas and turbans, and unisex items such as shoes with peep-toes and high heels. The man in the street thought he was bad news, and a disgrace to the upper class; while the socialists used him to gain a few votes. The female liberals, on the other hand, admired his originality, and scoffed at the biddies who suspected his lordship of being the leader of a cult that kidnapped and drugged the younger generation.

It was the rock-and-roll age. Rupert Gorhambury's antics began to seem restrained in comparison with the behaviour of pop people and football fans. He had a new name for Gorhambury, The Palace of Varieties, because he filled it with all sorts and conditions of men and women, heterosexuals, homosexuals, bisexuals, transexuals and hermaphrodites. He opened up the house to strangers on certain days until the police had to be called in once too often.

The charitable word was that he wrote books, or anyway was writing a book, and not wasting his time and his money on drugs and debauchery. Rosemary, his mother, who was allowed back into Gorhambury once a year without Nigel, proclaimed after her brief visits that he was working flat out and was deep into English literature, although she confessed tearfully to her husband that the place was a squalid dump and the inmates sat around spouting high-falutin gibberish. She revealed to Nigel that filthy pictures now hung in wall-spaces previously occupied by gentle watercolours painted by Victorian Widell spinsters and aunts.

Yet at long last, against expectations, ten years after Rupert had taken charge of his inheritance and his life, a book was produced. It was typical – that is, an oddity. Its title was: *Eve and I, by The Snake, with assistance from Old Adam and the Marquess of Gorhambury*. It claimed to be illustrated and its list of illustrations was titillating. The list ran: 'A wriggly introduction'; 'An apple from the teacher'; 'Where it is and how to get there'; 'The first arousal'; 'The first girl guide'; 'Two satisfied customers'; and 'Peace on earth – or was it an Armistice?' The illustrations in reality were modern and fashionable – they were mostly blank pages, white paper unsullied by pen, pencil, colour or printing. The frontispiece was again non-pictorial, but carried a subtitle: 'The intercourse to which you and I owe our existence.'

The text accompanying the illustrations that illustrated nothing was also up to date. It consisted of words, misspelt words, words unconnected, not sentences, not punctuated, not grammatical. For instance, the introduction began: 'Miday goldy sunbeans warmed laxury green dymantyne dazzle refillgence girl young girlie warm young sof sweet gold whirly-girl naked golded by sun on puby hair tensed snitched uplifted fit for luck and squeegeeing' – and so on.

The book was large, a hardback minus dust jacket bound in linen stamped with a gilded design of tracery in the Gothic style. The paper was thick and of fine quality, the type legible from a distance, and the publisher was The Palace of Varieties, Gorhambury, Gorham.

Rupert launched his book with the ball he had not given to celebrate his eighteenth birthday. He invited more than the thousand guests he had originally had in mind: they included press barons, the editors of every organ of news, the literary editors, the critics, the gossip columnists. The party became a media event before the invitations were sent out. Only four refusals arrived.

It was an extravaganza. An army of security men in camouflaged uniforms checked the invitation cards of guests in cars down by the lodge and iron gates into the park. The cars were then waved by security men into an area of level parkland some distance from the house: it was lit by flares. Golf-buggies ferried drivers and passengers to the tented approach to the front entrance: chauffeurs were directed to buses that would take them round to the back door and a separate place of entertainment. A red carpet had been laid across the gravel sweep to protect the priceless shoes of the ladies, and flood-lighting and the flickering light of flares created impressions of grandeur and festivity. In the marble halls women dripping with diamonds and scent, girls in costly rags dreamed up by shooting-star designers, superannuated nymphets girding their loins, and lesbians in dinner jackets and black bow ties, mingled with men in drag, in penguin suits, in ethnic kit, and in torn T-shirts and soiled jeans. Music played. In the ballrooms bands were both white and black, and everywhere the blaze of lights was as bewildering as the noise, music, smoke, drink and no doubt substances.

Rupert moved through the throng in the middle of a gang of his live-in playmates. He wore a silver suit and had glitter in his hair and on his cheeks, the others as various as possible sartorially, one in a burkha, another in a crinoline, a third in white tie and tails, a fourth in a leotard, a fifth in a tutu. The identifiable men were rather beautiful and one confusing figure had breasts and a beard.

212

Rupert smiled faintly on all and sundry and sometimes stopped to exchange a few words. Several of the newspaper people asked him about his book – where was it, when would they be getting it?

'In good time,' he murmured.

When journalists turned nasty – 'as is their wont', some cynic suggested – and a female feature writer said that Rupert might be a sodding Marquess but she would slay him if he did not grant her an exclusive interview, his gang closed ranks and swept on.

The hackneyed phrase, 'What a party!' was recycled and recirculated. Worldly people asked one another, 'What could it have cost?' Simpler souls chimed in, 'Aren't we lucky?' The curmudgeons accused their host of having more money than sense. The consensus of those who enjoyed and the others who sneered at his hospitality was that he must be deliciously pixilated or out of his mind.

But he was not so far out of it as some thought. When the guests prepared to leave the premises, they found their way blocked by the entire edition of his book and a counter complete with assistants and tills. Moreover men in camouflage were also there, carrying clipboards and walkie-talkies.

A critic was outraged when asked to buy one of the books for twenty pounds – he had expected to receive a free copy for review from his editor, and was not going to fork out a penny to swell the coffers of a multimillionaire. His name was taken, he was told with apologies that no buggy was available to transport him to his car parked a quarter of a mile away, and invited somewhat forcefully to wait on a nearby seat. He submitted, having noticed that it was raining. But then a departing guest bought a book and after a few minutes was ushered out under umbrellas to a buggy. And a gent and a lady appeared, bought three books and were instantly attended to. The critic protested, used the word blackmail, vowed revenge in print, and was kept waiting for three-quarters of an hour.

The first consequence of the great ball at Gorhambury was that most of the edition of *Eve and I* was bought on publication day or night. The second consequence was a storm in newsprint of denunciation of Rupert and mockery of his book. The third was still more dramatic.

His lordship hit back. He succeeded in persuading one titled owner of a national newspaper, who had not accepted his invitation, to give him the chance to respond to the adverse publicity: dog always eats dog in Fleet Street. Rupert's fellow-peer permitted him to reveal the names of all the journalists who had been at the ball: they were ungrateful, ill-mannered, philistine and corrupt, he wrote.

He posed a question in two parts: what right had he to jib at and object to the freedom of the press? And how dare he, how dare a mere marquess without qualifications or any democratic authorisation, attack the representatives of the

Fourth Estate, the pundits and the streetwise know-alls of the national media?

His answer was: because he had been attacked. His answers to both questions were that he was exceptional inasmuch as he had no need to kowtow and knuckle under to bullying; he had foreseen that the journalists he had chosen to invite to his ball would accept because they were every sort of snob, money and inverted and intellectual and fashion snobs, not averse to free fodder and booze, and in favour of kickbacks; that they would be bound to bite the hand which had fed them, also bound to do his book down because it was written by a gentleman and out of the ordinary, thus proving their commitment to the lowest common denominator in literature, culture, education, ethics and behaviour in general, all of which he aimed to correct.

Rupert continued: he himself was the publisher of his book because, in his estimation, it was too serious to be left to the whims of commerce. He had produced a collector's item and marketed it successfully – and cheaply, considering that every buyer had had a night out in glamorous surroundings with dinner and dancing thrown in. He ventured to claim that he had done a better job than was on offer from the retail book trade, which was motivated by a deep-seated distrust of originality and talent.

Rupert referred to the journalists' jeers at his title. Politicians and politicos were yet again peddling the snake oil of equality, of egalitarianism, and the classless society; but he had been discriminated against in print for having been born a marquess. He charged that his book was scorned for no other reason than that it was the work of a marquess. The critics chose to mis-understand his satire on the subject of modern art and pornography because a marquess had no right to comment on the pleasures of the pretentious, the poor, the vulgar and the stupid.

In short and in conclusion, he now had sufficient evidence to sue certain journalists and newspapers for damages caused by their concerted attempt to deny him his right to try to earn his living.

Rupert's book might not be good, judged by some standards; but his justification of it in a newspaper with a circulation of millions was a resounding success.

It was a rallying cry for a large section of the populace who detested critics of any description and especially critics in the first class seats of the gravy train of 'culsher'. In letters to Rupert, some made the shocking suggestion that literary editors asked only their cronies to write reviews, and reviewers reserved their praise for the outpourings of their friends and relations.

Bookworms and art-lovers seemed to want their marquess to strike a blow against hype and corruption, and even offered to contribute to the costs of the legal action.

He came to the High Court in lilac satin, a

suit cut like a military uniform with a neckband and frogging. He looked wan but composed, dignified but weedy and rather pathetic. The team of barristers acting for the media expected to make a meal of him.

His own barrister, supported by another team, asked for justice, neither more nor less, the same justice that would be meted out to a commoner who was prevented from earning the wages of his labour by slander and denigration in the market place.

The public gallery was full of Rupert's supporters, both playmates and strangers, who clapped and were rebuked by the judge.

The defendants' champion rose and spoke.

'Are you Rupert Theodore Widell, Baron Gorham and Marquess of Gorhambury?'

'I am.'

'Was your family name ever spelt differently?'

'It was.'

'Was it spelt "Widdle"?'

'Yes.'

'A strange name.'

'An accurate name.'

'Why accurate, Lord Gorhambury?'

'Because my family was endowed by the good God with the power to urinate on its enemies, such as yourself.'

The public gasped and laughed, the judge smiled and scolded, and the champion tried again.

'You are objecting to bad notices of a book – yes or no, if you please.'

'Yes.'

'A book called *Eve and I*?'

'Yes.'

'By "*A snake*"?'

'Yes.'

'Can snakes write?'

'Yes, with assistance from myself, as stated – the book is a fantasy, like Shakespeare's *The Tempest* or Lewis Carroll's *Lobster Quadrille*.'

'I would read part of a sentence composed by a snake and a marquess for this court's consideration. "Goldy sunbeans warmed ... sof sweet gold whirly-girl naked golded by sun on puby hair ... for luck and squeegeeing".'

There was laughter and a call for order.

'Is that sentence "writing", Lord Gorhambury?'

'Yes.'

'Indeed? By what standard do you arrive at such a conclusion?'

'By the highest standards applied by the so-called academic institutions of the present age.'

'Would you be kind enough to justify that statement?'

'Willingly. Permit me to read part of a sentence in my turn. "Leaning with the sloothering slide of her, giddygaddy, grannyma, gossipaceous..." It was written by an internationally acclaimed Irish writer, James Joyce.'

'James Joyce is a controversial figure, Lord Gorhambury.'

'So am I.'

More laughter in court.

The judge spoke.

218

'Continue with your questions, if you please.'

'Works of art, Lord Gorhambury – would you say that the frontispiece of your work was a work of art? It is a page of unmarked white paper.'

Rupert's barrister was signalled to and held up a painter's canvas coloured blue.

Rupert asked: 'Is that picture a work of art?'

The champion objected and was overruled. The judge requested elucidation.

'What point are you making, Lord Gorhambury?'

'It's a painting by Smolkins.'

'Who is Smolkins?'

'A modern artist.'

'It looks like nothing on earth.'

'With respect, my lord, you are looking at five hundred thousand pounds of value.'

After more laughter the judge nodded at the champion, who remarked: 'Some fool might pay so much for a picture like that, but money does not make it a work of art any more than your money, since you paid for the production of your book, makes its frontispiece a work of art.'

Rupert addressed the judge: 'May I read one sentence from an article by Sir Nicolas Green, our foremost art historian and critic, knighted for his services to British painting?'

'Proceed.'

'Sir Nicholas has described the picture you have seen, *Blue Lagoon*, in these terms: "It is a glowing representation of the essence of nature, comparable with the great works of a previous age, for instance by John Constable." I can supply the name of the periodical in which Sir Nicholas wrote, and the date of the relevant issue.'

The judge spoke to the champion of journalism, who was mopping his brow: 'Do you have more questions?'

'I do, your honour. Lord Gorhambury, you gave a party to launch your book?'

'Not exactly, sir.'

'How so?'

'I gave a ball on my birthday, my book was launched on the same evening, and I invited some newspaper people along who might have been interested in it.'

'I put it to you that you invited critics to your party in hopes of getting them to review your book.'

'No, sir. I did not expect them to review my book well, because I am a marquess and they would not wish to appear to be licking my boots, nor did I expect them to review it at all, since they were not and never would be friends of mine.'

'I will ignore your slur on the integrity of critics, and put it to you that you were trying to bribe journalists to advertise your book?'

'No, sir. I had no need to buy advertisement. I was sure my book would create a stir. And sure enough you and your paymasters have given me more free publicity than I could possibly have paid for.'

Laughter again, and slightly less stern words from the judge.

'Lord Gorhambury,' the champion began again, 'copies of your book were sold at your party?'

'Some of my guests wished to buy a copy.'

'Setting aside the legal aspect of such trade, was it not close-fisted of you, a wealthy man, to force your guests to pay the full retail price of your book?'

'My guests were entertained at a cost of one hundred pounds a head, they paid twenty pounds per copy of my book. Accounts are available.'

'You compelled my clients to buy a book apiece. They were not offered transport to their cars until they had done so. I can call witnesses to substantiate the charge of compulsion.'

'I can call witnesses, too, sir. I have no power over booksellers, unlike your clients, who were unlikely to review or notice my book, which would therefore not be stocked in bookshops. Moreover I was disinclined to give away a hundred and fifty copies of the edition of one thousand of my book, the customary hundred and fifty for journalists, since it's well-known that literary editors and critics supplement their incomes by selling review copies whether or not they have reviewed the books. My guests found my book on sale and bought nearly the whole edition, I am happy to report. They were then driven to their cars, which they had parked on my land, and my staff recorded no complaints. Inevitably some guests were delayed – a thousand couldn't be taken to their cars simultaneously; but the stories they have published, alleging force and compulsion, seem to be afterthoughts, and are still being looked at by my lawyers who specialise in slander.'

The judge allowed a few more questions and answers, then interrupted impatiently. He said the case was a storm in a teacup, was wasting his own time and the time of the judiciary. He demanded final and brief submissions from both parties.

The champion thundered and whinged that the gravest charges had been levelled against the media, and he was not being allowed his chance to rebut them. Businessmen of international renown, publishers of worldwide significance, great newspapers and illustrious journalists were under attack from a marquess, who had made an exhibition of his frivolity and perverse idea of humour not only in his book and his malicious broadsheet article, but also in the dress he affected, the satin dress, which was disrespectful of the court. He begged that substantial damages should be awarded to his clients, the legitimate representatives of our literary traditions and history and the guardians of the most precious boon of our constitution, an unfettered press.

Rupert's barrister read out passages from the reviews and gossip column inches *Eve and I* and its author had received: that the book was decadent, disgraceful, sickening, an affront, an onslaught on the British way of life, punishable by law or by vigilante action, and that the writer richly deserved the metaphorical and indeed the literal punishment of the nearest lamp-post.

The judge awarded a hundred pounds to

Rupert and his costs to the other side – the media were liable for half a million all told.

Shortly after the publication of *Eve and I*, the court case, and sell-out of the book's first and second printings, an unusual event occurred at Gorhambury: twins were born.

Babies galore had been born there in recent years. Girls in Rupert Gorhambury's entourage often gave birth. But this time was different. Twins were different. Twin boys were also exceptional, and their mother was out of the ordinary. She was a promiscuous clever woman, Daphne, surname unknown, who drifted into Gorhambury, dressed Middle Eastern, and had concealed the fact that she was pregnant. Her labour verged on the magical. She disappeared one morning and reappeared at dinner with a babe in each arm. She had summoned a friend who was a midwife in West Ashe, the friend had entered the house without being noticed, and had already left unnoticed. Mother and sons all seemed well and strong. Another extraordinary circumstance was that parturition had run its course in Rupert's own four-poster bed. And the concomitant revelation that caused most amazement and distress was Daphne's claim that he was the twins' father.

Rupert, even before being accused of fatherhood, was a nervous wreck. His constitution had always been shaky and unreliable. He seemed to have used up nearly his whole lifetime's store of energy in producing *Eve and I* and in the subsequent events. He was at a low ebb when Daphne dumped the twins in his lap when he was expecting a cup of nourishing soup.

Dinner was a group ritual. At least fifteen people were seated at the refectory table in the Great Hall of Gorhambury, and butler Hopkins and parlour-maid Nelly were serving the first course, when Daphne made her entrance. Hubbub as chairs fell backwards, exclamations, congratulations ensued, and Daphne was made to rest and swallow soup on a convenient sofa.

When the babies had ceased to bawl and peace was more or less restored, Rupert protested in a tearful voice: 'They can't be mine.'

Stronger drinks than soup were called for. The rest of the meal was eaten in a rush, since everybody was eager for Hopkins and Nelly to be out of the way, whether or not they were out of earshot. At last the desired discussion began with Daphne swearing on strange divinities that her twins were Widells and one of them was also Lord Bushton and would be the Marquess of Gorhambury one fine day. Rupert denied it, although he admitted that he shared his bed frequently, had shared it off and on with Daphne, and that owing to his intake of drugs, sleeping pills, wake-up pills and painkillers he might not have known what he was doing or what was being done to him.

At this point Gerry, a sculptor of a certain age who had appropriated the Orangery for his studio, boasted that intimacy had occurred when he was modelling a figurine of Daphne in the altogether: it was just about nine months ago, a gardener might have noticed because they would have been visible through the windows, and anyway he was sure his seed was more potent than whatever was or was not supplied by Rupert. Daphne roused herself to rebut this claim. She had armed herself with a contraceptive before entering the Orangery as Gerry was such a goat. Besides, none of the dates tallied, and she trusted her contraceptive more than she trusted any man.

Then Anthony, the medievalist, who was also resident at Gorhambury, confessed that he and Daphne had made love in the sacristy of St Sebastian's church in Foxham, where they had gone to rub brasses. He said he would be happy to assume responsibility for the little boys. But Daphne said their love had only been fooling, and had got nowhere. The drama turned farcical when Simon also put his oar in: Simon, half-poet and half-nitwit, said he thought he had had Daphne too, an assumption which she rejected with as much force as she could muster amidst general laughter.

Rupert took to his bed. The prospect of paternity, the possibility that he was being plucked, unmanned him completely. But after two or three days he rallied and, with playmates in tow, limped along to see the mother and children, who had established themselves in one of the old nurseries.

Daphne welcomed him. She could do crossword

puzzles and had gained a first class degree in Media Studies, but was an untidy careless cuddly woman. The nursery was in a mess and she seemed to be too disorganised to grind an axe.

'I won't ever marry you,' Rupert shrilled at her.

'No, dear, of course you won't, I don't expect it,' she replied.

He argued briefly that he still believed he was a virgin – he had always played Queen Elizabeth the First in the Gorhambury charades – and that a spot of petting could not have amounted to impregnation.

She inquired: 'Does it matter?'

Her arguments were that she jolly well should know better than he did, because she had worked harder and longer than he had at the insemination, and now two beautiful boys had come into the world, the Widell family had a future, she would probably move on according to her custom in a short while, and she just hoped her little ones would not be thrown on to the streets.

His argument was beside those particular points. He was convinced that she was not lying, although she could be wrong. And he was inclined to be a father, after all. But he remembered James and John, twins and ancestors, who between them had created havoc, and he was worried that history might repeat itself.

Daphne said: 'Oh, that's another bridge – there's a long way to go before you're there – wait and see would be my advice – look what you've gone and done without even knowing it.'

He relented. He went to register the birth after a celebratory lunch, at which he decided to call the older twin Oscar after Oscar Wilde and the younger, because he could think of nothing better, Theodore Rupert Valentine. When the Registrar asked for the name of the father of the child, he answered: 'Various.' He was not allowed to get away with it, and eventually his own name was entered on the document alongside that of their mother, who had insisted on being written in as Daphne Goodbody, spinster.

The strain of recent events was too much for Rupert, and his frail mental health broke down. The Marchioness of Gorhambury and her husband Nigel Bagmold had to be summoned, and they and his doctors spirited him away to a special hospital, where he languished for a year. His revival was as odd as his previous life had been: it was a reversion. He was transformed from a playboy in satin, from an amoral nihilist and wastrel, into a squire in a tweed suit and a collar and tie, who wore brown brogues and a flat cap out of doors.

He returned to Gorhambury and was appalled by what he found there, although nothing had changed so much as he had. He had become allergic to people in the plural and noise, and he asked his playmates to find alternative accommodation. They resisted. They had nowhere to go and no money. They were not criminals, they were lost souls and flotsam.

Rupert asked his solicitors for money, a round sum, one million pounds, and his solicitors, now

Messrs Drewett, Block and Carter, asked for an urgent meeting.

They met at Gorhambury.

'My lord,' Mr Drewett began after the usual polite preamble, 'may we ask for what purpose the million pounds is required?'

'You may not,' Rupert replied with his new-found firmness and authority.

Mr Drewett blinked in a pained manner behind his hornrims.

Mr Block gazed at his lordship through his rimless glasses and, true to his name, said in a reproachful tone of voice: 'A million pounds is a great deal of spending money, Lord Gorhambury.'

'Gentlemen,' Rupert replied, 'I read three messages in your six eyes, and I cannot say I like any of them.'

The solicitors were puzzled.

Mr Carter inquired: 'Messages, my lord?'

'Objections, to be precise.'

A lawyer-like chorus greeted the explanation: 'Surely not … There was no intention … We await instructions, Lord Gorhambury.'

'The trio of objections I have seen in your eyes are death and duty and better not, which I take to mean that you want to hold on to my million to pay the duty on my death, which cannot be long delayed.'

Another chorus of negatives turned into a refrain of second thoughts and affirmatives.

Rupert said, 'Thank you, gentlemen,' and in due course received his million.

He redistributed it. He paid to be left in peace. He gave away the wherewithal to live and to die on, houses, flats, annuities, pensions.

As a result, Daphne, Miss Goodbody, was sorry to see his playmates who were also hers go their separate ways. She missed them, was lonely, and tired of nappies and one-sided conversations with giggles and boohoos. She reminded Rupert that she was never one to gather moss, and requested leave to roll on: she knew he would care for Oscar and Theodore better than she could.

He said: 'Yes, yes,' and wrote her a bumper cheque with relief. They were not intimates, whether or not intimacy had ever occurred, and she was an embarrassing reminder of the slap-happy morality and sloppiness of his earlier years. He felt lucky to be getting rid of her, and then doubly lucky to find a nanny for the boys, Nanny Bates, who had a motherly appearance and a strong and upright character.

He had realised the aims of what he regarded as his second incarnation. He was tidying up Gorhambury little by little, and rendering it respectable. He could allow his mother and Nigel to come to tea in the reconstituted drawing-room. Apart from the twins, Nanny Bates, the parlour-maid Nelly, and the other servants who had never deserted their posts under fire from all the aggravation, he was on his own. He himself kept his flag flying: shaved, had his hair cut, dressed properly, tried to eat meals at the appointed hours, also to attend to urgent business, and succumbed to bed in between times. He admitted his doctor, although they both knew his health was deteriorating and nothing much could be done – his heart was weak, and weakened his lungs, kidneys, and whole constitution. He was not sorry, he was almost content. He looked back at the excesses of his past with wonder. He toyed with books, watched anodyne TV, dreamed and roamed through the gilded space and long corridors of his empty palace. At night he switched lights on and off in attics and the bachelor wing, and in domestic offices in the basement. For company, he had the ghosts of his predecessors.

His most precious time was spent in the nursery. He loved his twins, and struggled in vain not to make too obvious a favourite of the elder. He believed the impossible: that Oscar was his without doubt. The child was fair, blue-eyed, fragile and wistful – Rupert saw himself when he gazed at Oscar, another version of himself, pure and with nothing to be ashamed of. He confided in Oscar who listened and did not answer back. He whispered into his cot in the evenings.

'Our family would be going down the drain, but for you,' he said. 'We did not deserve you, truth to tell, because you were begat by magic. I'm effete – that's the word for me – overbred, overpaid, and under-equipped in every department. I made a sort of name for myself in the easiest way, by scandalising people. I even won a round or two in the fisticuffs of existence, but

I lost by winning, I was a nobody who had no heart for becoming somebody. So be it! I'm a fatalist – to be anything except a fatalist is silly. I'm learning from you, Oscar, because you know all because you know nothing. What will you become? You'll do well if you grow up to be nothing like me. Anyway, I wish you well, my dear.'

Square One

The blessings of the second pair of Widell twins
– the blessings that *were* these twins in the
opinions of many – wore impenetrable disguises
in the experience of a few, the family solicitors,
for example, and persons with long memories
still employed by the Estate, and old retainers
and local businesses and institutions dependent
on the bounty of their lordships.

Rupert, fifth Marquess, died as he had foreseen.
Unfortunately he died intestate. He forgot the
urgings of Drewett, Block and Carter to make
testamentary arrangements, therefore exposed his
loved one, Oscar, his infant heir, the sixth
Marquess, to the depredations of an Inland
Revenue red in tooth and claw. A huge chunk
of the estate, money, land, property, including
works of art, were subject to the tax called Death
Duty.

The lawyers, led by the stepfather of the
deceased, Bagmold by name, sought to minimise
the damage. They argued points with the tax
collectors. Again unfortunately, thanks to the
complications of the family finances and the
ineradicable and inexcusable delays of the law,
they overlooked the health of the child they

were working for. Three years after Rupert's death, when they had finalised the amount of tax payable, a slightly lower figure than had at first been demanded, and incidentally ran up fees comparable with the savings, Oscar died of meningitis, and a second chunk of Death Duty was demanded.

Once more the lawyers buckled on their breastplates and reached for their battleaxes. They fought the Commissioners of Inland Revenue from review to review, from one court to another, and years passed, ten years in the end. Bagmold passed on, or rather up, to argue his case before St Peter. Drewett retired to a stately mansion he had been able to buy in the Goatacre region. Block invested in a second home near St Tropez, and Carter also did well and grew fat. The new team in the old firm were Carter, Bream and Hemming. All were satisfied to have brought the Gorhambury case to a conclusion, even if the owner, the seventh Marquess, was not far from ruination.

He, the seventh Marquess, the younger twin called Theodore, was fifteen when the lawyers brought him the mixed bag of their news. He was one of those twins which are the opposite of identical: in fact it had occurred to his putative father, despite the impossibility, that Gerry, the virile sculptor, could have been half-right – his seed could have squirmed past Daphne's contraceptive device.

Theodore at fifteen was a fine specimen of boyhood or youth or early manhood, upstanding, well built, with rosy cheeks and steady blue eyes, clearly energetic and eager. His complexion had the brown tint of his namesake, the first Theodore, and his brown hair was springy. He already had a touch of distinction. Undoubtedly, beyond all doubts, he had the look of a thoroughbred and a gentleman.

He had been shielded from the vicissitudes of his life to date, the disappearance of his mother, deaths of his father and his brother, and the legal wrangle over his inheritance. His grand-mother and her husband Bagmold had prevailed upon the family lawyers with the power of attorney to protect the boy from fatalities and tax gatherers. Theodore was enabled to go to the schools his forebears had gone to, and in his holidays at Gorhambury, where Nanny Bates was in *loco parentis*, he rode his pony, learned to shoot with his gamekeeper, entertained his local contemporaries to tea, tennis, hide-and-seek in the grounds and games of Murder indoors on winter evenings, and was invited to similar parties in return. His best luck to date, not counting the marquessate and the barony, was that he had a strong constitution and a sunny temperament.

In his sixteenth year, he returned home for the summer holidays, and was visited by three men, not necessarily wise men, his solicitors.

Mr Carter, the senior partner, ran through the sorry tale of the family's impoverishment.

He ended: 'Gorhambury is yours, my lord, and your income now derives from your houses in London which are let at rewarding rents. The income can pay for outgoings, wages for a few employees, an allowance for yourself, and the fees for our services, which, I would emphasise, are minimal. The rest of the London property has been sold, and the same applies to the estate. Regretfully, we have to tell you that the costs of your schooling are under threat – we cannot afford them without further sales, which in turn would reduce your income and your prospects. We are therefore convinced that decisions have to be taken, and would value your opinion and advice, my lord. We are sorry to bear bad news, but I think we can fairly claim that your present predicament is no fault of ours, sir.'

Theodore replied: 'I'm not blaming you, Mr Carter, and wouldn't, because we authorised you to act on our behalf, and nobody can prevail against death and taxes. One essential decision I can take straight away. I shall not go back to school, and would be grateful if you would inform the headmaster and my housemaster. I'm not a scholar, and for some time I've felt I was wasting time and money on impractical lessons. I'd rather learn a trade, and do my best to hang on to Gorhambury and attend to my responsibilities here.'

The three solicitors were impressed by his speech, and hurried back to their offices to re-check the accounts which Lord Gorhambury might attend to.

Theodore dealt with his predicament realistically and without nostalgia. He worked at correcting what was wrong with Gorhambury and the remnants of the old estate. He plugged holes in the roof, unblocked drains and gutters, filled in potholes in the drive and helped to dig the garden. He answered calls for help from his tenants: their roofs were also leaking. He signed on for night classes in plumbing and carpentry at the West Ashe Technical College, calling himself Rupert Valentine and dropping his surname.

He was busy, he was uncomplaining, but he was not making money. Nanny Bates still lived in the former nurseries, and Eileen and Mary, respectively resident cook and housekeeper in the palmy days, now came in daily, and the odd-job man John mowed the lawns and battled with the garden. Theodore, with their agreement and assistance, began to offer bed and breakfast in part of Gorhambury to a passing trade. The public trooped in, younger staff had to be engaged, and in summer dinner with the Marquess was also on offer. It was a decent little business that attracted publicity and was profitable; but, again, the profits were drops in the ocean of his financial requirements.

The fabric of Gorhambury, and its structure, were deteriorating. There were rising damp in the lower floors and dry rot on a back staircase, a completely new roof was needed, the Bachelor Wing was subsiding, and the lake had been taken over by weed and water lilies. Estimated cost of all repairs was in the region of three million. And another million or two should be spent on the London houses, on the cottages where ex-servants of the Widells lived rent-free, also on the Widell almshouses, and places like the Town Hall and the Cottage Hospital, which the Widells had built and the bricks and mortar of which they were in principle obliged to maintain.

Theodore at seventeen dreamed of selling up. He consulted his solicitors, who told him that property prices had slumped, derelict stately homes were a drug on the market, no buyer was likely to shoulder the burden of the vendor's historic duties, and he would come up against other problems by selling and be subject to widespread criticism.

He soldiered on without seeing much light at the end of the tunnel. He was too idealistic to seek relief where some of his forefathers had found it, in the arms of an heiress. He told cynical friends he did not know any heiresses, and that heiresses did not stay in bed-and-breakfast accommodation. His grandmother, Rosemary, was unhelpful: in her opinion he was neither to sell Gorhambury nor to stay there and wait on unappreciative tourists.

Nanny Bates said all along, 'You never know,' and she was proved more right than the others.

When Theodore was nineteen he received a personal letter from the USA. Its arrival was startling, its contents likewise. The typewritten script laid claim to a relationship with himself, and was signed Hiram Widdle. Mr Widdle had long ago seen a report of Theodore's father's court case, noticed the original surname of the Widells, believed or hoped that he was related to them, was now retired and coming to England on business, and would very much like to make the acquaintance of the Marquess of Gorhambury and visit at his very lovely home.

Theodore replied politely and on an appointed afternoon Mr Widdle rang his doorbell. He was a small pudgy man in late middle age, balding, bespectacled, and wearing a sports jacket of thin loudly checked material and a baseball cap. Mrs Widdle was smaller than he was but powerfully built, with gleaming white teeth, and also dressed in sports gear although she must have been in her sixties, a tight T-shirt and slacks with pockets in unlikely places. She carried a bag that looked as if it was meant for the week's shopping.

Theodore showed them round. He did not deny or endorse their cousinship: to deny might have seemed churlish, and it would have been rude to suggest that his visitor was another descendant of a foundling. Conversation during the tour he conducted was sticky as both Widdles were reduced to silence by the size of the house and the rooms: they opened their mouths only to utter monosyllables such as 'My!' and 'Wow!' But over tea Mr Widdle came out with an electrifying question.

'How much are you asking for it?'

'Excuse me?' Theodore inquired.

'No, sir, you excuse me, please, for noticing the state of this building – it looks to me like the old world's waiting for a little assistance from the new. Would you consider selling it lock, stock and barrel to a relative?'

'It wasn't for sale, Mr Widdle.'

'We have a proverb in the States, sir – everything's for sale at the right price.'

'But Gorhambury would be priceless – it's one of the biggest houses in Europe – I haven't thought seriously of selling it.'

'Well, sir, I'm a chemist, and I've made more money than I know what to do with. My business is agricultural and horticultural fertiliser, and my patent allows me to process all animal waste products. You name your price if you decide to sell your residence. And I'll call you in one week from today to hear your yay or nay.'

Theodore bade them goodbye. He did not let on that he was ready with his yay. He felt as if a weight had been lifted from the top of his head and he was suddenly inches taller. He summoned Mr Carter.

He had to give his solicitor alcoholic refreshment. They both resorted to strong liquor. He explained: he had almost abandoned hope of climbing out of the financial hole he was in, and he was no longer willing to be enslaved by a cause already lost. As for tradition and auld lang syne, he was not much moved by stuff of that sort. He was apparently in receipt of a windfall, and he was not going to reject it and cling on for somebody else to wave a wand and save his bacon.

The price that Theodore agreed with Mr Widdle cleared his debts, gave him private means,

240

safeguarded the interests of his tenants and employees, and included money for the charities supported by his family.

Theodore smiled inwardly to think that he and Hiram Widdle were linked if not exactly related by their indebtedness to bodily functions.

A handsome teenage Marquess willing to run a B and B, who was forced by reasons beyond his control to abandon his home, Gorhambury, a jewel in the crown of the English landscape, an historical landmark, a centre of local employment, escaped censure from the majority. He was only criticised to his face by his grandmother, who said he had sold his birthright to a Yankee maker of muck in bulk. He laughed at her, and shook the dust of the wide lands of the Widells off his shoes.

He removed to a flat in London, in Westminster, close to the Houses of Parliament. He knew that, in an era of inverted snobbery, a lordling would find it more difficult to get a decent job than the man in the street, and he was unwilling to be thrown the sop of a sinecure in exchange for the use of his name. But he had work waiting for him in the House of Lords, and as soon as possible he donned his family's red robes trimmed with ermine and took his seat amongst his fellow peers.

He was interested in politics, he seemed to have been born with a weakness for knotty problems, and he liked to think that practicality was another of his middle names. Perhaps he resembled the first Marquess of Gorhambury, who had brought his common sense to bear in Victorian back rooms. Theodore the seventh Marquess was also as non-party-political as the first, and proved his independence by not sitting on the benches to the right and the left of the central aisle in the Chamber. He postponed his maiden speech; but his youth combined with his other significant characteristics won him places on committees. Before long he was doing the bidding of his noble elders and betters and running their errands.

Society, the society called 'high', scented its prey. He was hunted to a standstill and dragged into that other world ruled by rich women. He was mobilised by the charitable brigade. He was invited everywhere. He made the acquaintance of adult fun, which, translated into the language of reality, boils down to sex in more or less respectable forms and surroundings.

Theodore in his early twenties had spent ten minutes now and again with prostitutes. He was ready to be romantic at the right time, but he was not sentimental. He hoped to marry a good girl, and did not stoop to suspecting every debutante of wanting to be a marchioness.

At a ball he was made aware of the existence of Bee, a seasoned debutante, not in her first youth, twenty-two years old, a tall smiling brunette with slightly sticking-out teeth. They danced together. At another ball they danced closer. In between dances they laughed a lot. And she told him she had accommodation of her own in London, a flat in a West End block. After another social engagement he drove her to her address, and she did not immediately get out of his car. They kissed; they formed an addiction to kissing; in the days and nights that followed they kissed in parks, doorways, back alleys, everywhere. After their fifth or sixth encounter, she invited him into her flat when they had dined in a restaurant, and they were as near as nothing lovers in a technical sense.

Bee – short for Beatrice, Beatrice Wallace – worked as receptionist in a shop selling smart cars. It was not a demanding job, all she had to do was to dress well and smile at the customers, and she was satisfied to do it. She looked bemused if he spoke of his work in the House of Lords. She liked to hear about Gorhambury, and was awfully sad it was sold. She read magazines and middle-brow bestsellers. She watched soap operas on TV and programmes showing gory operations in hospitals. She had girlfriends galore; she was apt to receive calls on her mobile from one or another of them when she was out with Theodore.

There had been a pause as if for thought after the narrow squeak in her flat. He had drawn back and perhaps she had too. He argued inwardly that she was decorative, amicable, jolly, well-connected in class terms. She knew the social and, it seemed, the sexual ropes. She was not an awkward or neurotic person. She would be an undemanding wife, so long as her demands – for a good time and to be spared problems –

were supplied. But she would not be his helpmeet. She showed no sign of being able or willing to meet him halfway intellectually. She was not deep and was lacking in imagination. In short, she was all very well, but not the girl of his dreams.

The most compelling of arguments on the other hand could be compressed into two words: physical attractions. Moreover, restraint and postponement, if not exactly absence, did make Theodore's heart grow fonder. He was enjoying the titillation of whether or not to commit himself. Between the two of them a sort of mounting tension lent dramatic force to their relationship.

Bee invited Theodore to accompany her to the home of a friend of hers for the weekend. He hesitated, then agreed. Bee's friend was a giggler called Dolly Courthope and her home was a renovated castle in Kent and her parents were abroad. It was a young party, Dolly's live-in lover Tim was included, and a Jimmy ditto with Rosie, and a Herman with Alexis – they were eight in all. The castle teemed with staff, and the conventions were respected to the extent of no shared bedrooms and not turning up late or in jeans for dinner on the first – Saturday – evening.

Theodore felt out of place nonetheless, and his excitement of finding himself allotted the dressing-room with a connecting door to Bee's bedroom was also a worry. He had nothing much in common with the other unknown guests. To begin with he was embarrassed to feel that his status was casting a blight over a reunion of old friends, and then he wished the old friends were rather more reined in by his presence. They drank deep of Mr Courthope's wines and the volume of their voices increased proportionately. They shouted and screamed at one another across the dining-room table, and flicked bread pellets. In the drawing-room after dinner pop music was played too loud, Herman and Alexis tried to dance and fell over, Dolly and Tim performed a funny tango, and the conversation sank to the level of swearing and rude noises, which amused most of the company.

Not late, although Theodore had been sure his watch was going slow, Mr Courthope's authoritative butler informed Dolly that he was about to switch on the burglar alarm and the party would have to retire to the upper floor. Bee held Theodore's hand on the stairs and wrapped it round her waist – she was tipsy and in need of support. Eventually the dawdling in the passages was done and he escorted her into her bedroom. She apologised for the evening – 'Not your scene, darling' – and added by way of compensation with a saucy glance, 'But the night's still young.'

'No, Bee—'

She stopped his mouth with kisses.

He broke away and said firmly that she was not in a fit state and he was not in the mood to play. She slumped on to her bed and pouted at him in a disappointed manner, and he kissed her good night chastely, went into his bedroom and shut the connecting door.

He changed into pyjamas, put on a dressing-gown, and crossed the passage to a bathroom. On his return to his room he could hear Bee cleaning her teeth in the bathroom adjoining her bedroom. He would have been more sorely tempted if he had not guessed that she was tipsily out to seduce him. He was determined not to gamble his entire life on a girl the worse for drink. He gritted his teeth and wished he had had the nerve to lock both his doors.

She burst in. She was naked and she carried the lamp from her bedside switched on. She was laughing and saying: 'Spotlight on charm!' He said, 'No, no, no,' and approached with the intention of evicting her from his room. She drew away from him in a mixture of flirting and mock terror, and said: 'On approval – reserved for my husband!'

He pushed her out with her lamp and now locked the door. His night was disturbed not by Bee but by himself, and for a mixture of physical and ethical reasons. Breakfast was scheduled for nine o'clock; and Theodore washed, shaved, dressed, hearing no sign of life from next door, and went downstairs punctually. The others were more or less late and hungover, and Bee was the last down at about half past ten. She looked unwell and drank black coffee and avoided Theodore's eye. When Dolly had dragged Tim to the village church, and Jimmy and Rosie and Herman and Alexis had settled down with the Sunday papers, he asked Bee to come out for a breath of air.

They promenaded in the extensive garden and he said: 'I'm leaving here soon, I'm going to tell Dolly I've been called back to London for an urgent business meeting.'

'Is it because of me?' she asked in an unsteady voice.

'No, because of me, because I've decided there's no future for us, and I wanted to ask you to forgive me for letting things go on for as long as they have.'

'Did I behave very badly last night?'

'Very seductively.'

'Are you saying goodbye, Theodore?'

'Yes.'

She cried.

'It's sad for both of us,' he murmured, handing her his handkerchief.

'Oh well, it was nice while it lasted,' she volunteered.

'Nicer than that,' he corrected her.

'I was a fool, I got carried away by our rooms being so close, I'm the one who needs forgiving for losing my head and not knowing sooner that I was too foolish for you.'

'Thanks for everything, Bee.'

They hugged each other.

He said: 'We'll go indoors, you can disappear, I'll do a telephone call, tell everyone I'm off and explain why.'

Time passed. Two years passed. Theodore concentrated on his work and steered as clear as he could of the stumbling blocks and pitfalls of society and sex. He heard that Beatrice Wallace was conducting tours in the Himalayas, and then, thankfully, that she was engaged to marry a military man. But his life was void of tenderness. He was near to despairing of ever meeting his soulmate.

She seemed to step out of his dream. He met her in the summer, at a cocktail party on the terrace on the river side of the Houses of Parliament. She was American, a distant relation of a member of the delegation of Senators and Congressmen who were being entertained by their British counterparts. She had taken the place of the wife of her cousin, Senator Burnett – Mrs Burnett was unwell. She was actually travelling round Europe alone, sightseeing. She was young and blonde, with wide-apart eyes and perfect teeth, vital, vigorous, curious and dignified. Her name was Constance, a good omen.

She asked him: 'Are you very important here?'

'I'm a dogsbody,' he replied.

She believed him, or almost. He invited her to lunch and would tell her no more than that his first name was Theo. Her family farmed in Colorado, and she had a brother called Hank. He escorted her to see some of the sights on her list, Kew Gardens and Keats' house in Hampstead. He had fallen in love at first sight, but every moment in her company reinforced his love. She was sweet to him but not forward. She had a sense of humour and of the ridiculous, also an interest in practical matters that matched his own. She was earnest, aspiring to learn and improve herself, which touched him and charmed. She was always a woman, not giddy and never forward.

He declared his love this time, impulsively, unavoidably, fearing it was too soon; and she was covered in confusion, blushing, tearful, laughing and saying she was not worthy.

He could not have imagined anyone better than she was, or anything, for that matter. They kissed – her kisses were poetic. Wonder and thrills were the order of their days. But she was moving on – she had bookings to travel to Venice and stay there, and loved ones at home, anxious that all was well and looking forward to her return. He had to hurry. They had seen so little of each other – no more than a few hours spread over a week – and still she knew him only by his Christian name, by part of his Christian name: before it was too late he had to be honest, and perhaps foolhardy.

One evening they strolled hand in hand along the Albert Embankment opposite the Houses of Parliament, which she had expressed a wish to see properly. She spoke of her upbringing on the farm near Colorado Springs, and, in a sort of swap of personal information, he pointed across the river and said: 'I belong there.'

She misunderstood: she thought he had meant just that he worked in the building.

'I'm a member of the House of Lords,' he said.

She was nonplussed.

'How come?'

'Because my father and forefathers were lords.'

'What's your name, Theo?'

'Gorhambury.'

He had to spell it and coach her with the pronunciation.

'Oh my!' she said.

'That's not all,' he continued. 'I'm a marquess, too.'

'What's your full name, then?'

He laughed and said: 'Are you ready to be surprised?'

'And waiting.'

'Very well. I'm the thirteenth Baron Gorham, Lord Gorham, that is, and the seventh Marquess of Gorhambury, commonly known as Lord Gorhambury.'

'Mercy!'

'It makes not the slightest difference to me, and I'm hoping and praying it won't make too much difference to you, because I'm normal in other respects or think so, and I've never known such a splendid person as you are, I love you with all my heart, and I'd be honoured and my life would be transformed for the better if you would consent to be my wife.'

She was overcome, fanned her face with her hand, and clung to him either by way of answer or to hold herself upright. He guided her towards a seat, and they remained in a long embrace while they whispered questions and answers, endearments, and nothings sweet enough but boiling down to her plea for time to consider his proposal which, she said, must be as extraordinary as an American girl ever did receive.

The proprieties were observed. No liberties were taken on either side. They were either old-fashioned or ahead of the worn-out and witless phase of free sex and its calamities. She granted him one encouraging favour. She agreed that he could follow and be with her, though not in the same hotel, in Venice.

They travelled and spent ten days always together. As the Venetian nights fell, in the moon's light, Theodore managed to hold back by reminding himself of the fable of the tortoise and the hare. They talked things over endlessly and sensibly, but at least with the laughter linked to present excitement and future joy.

She said: 'I'd die if I had to call myself a marchioness.'

'You'd get used to it.'

'Not in the USA, my friends would tease me, I'd never stop blushing, I'd have to be your missis.'

'If you like – why not in America? – but at home, in this country, be careful not to show you're embarrassed by the title, because if you do other girls will think you're shamming – all the snobs will be down on you for pretending to spurn what they envy.'

She also said: 'I wouldn't like to compete with the English girls and be hated for winning.'

'I know no English girls.'

'Didn't you warn me that I might be envied?'

'You must be envied already.'

'Thank you, but seriously, Theo – I suppose you're grand and rich?'

'I'm neither. Snobs probably think I'm grand, and fools that I'm rich. I've told you that Gorhambury is mine no longer, and I have a private income but have to earn in order to make ends meet. If you married me I'd accept offers of menial jobs and we'd manage.'

'Do you want to do menial jobs?'

'Not much – but I might be offered a directorship. I've been offered directorships once or twice – and I'd accept now in order to feed my family.'

On the subject of money she said: 'Could I keep my bank account in my maiden name?'

He replied: 'What would the bank clerks imagine if a marquess was paying money regularly into the account of Miss Constance Burnett?'

The difficulty was overcome – other difficulties likewise. She spoke to her parents on the telephone, and she spoke to Hank and a couple of girlfriends. On their last Sunday in Venice they attended a service in St Mark's, and during it, in the dark interior, while the choir sang, she tugged his sleeve and, when he turned to look in her shiny eyes, she said: 'Yes, if you haven't changed your mind.'

They were married in the Chapel at Gorhambury – Hiram Widdle insisted on it – and their marriage was blessed in the church in Wagonway, the village in the shadow of the Rocky Mountains near Burnett Holding, the farm where Constance's family had lived and worked for a century. Her parents Jim and Alice Burnett, and her brother Hank, took to Theodore and vice versa; and all Constance's other relations and her friends made him welcome.

The couple lived in Theodore's Westminster flat, which was sufficiently roomy even after first Anthony Bushton, then Thomas Widell, were born. Constance spent time intermittently with her new family in Colorado, taking one son, taking two, and her husband if possible; and her mother visited and again helped her with the children. The little boys were sturdy and intelligent.

The marriage was all that both parties had trusted it would be. Theodore and Constance, notwithstanding their separate nationalities, their divergent beginnings, and linguistic variations, were compatible and comfortable with each other. They were more than that, but they preferred the mundane practical description of their happiness. They were homebodies – they had more fun together at home than in social settings or with hordes of merrymakers. When she was in the USA and he was stuck in London, he read widely in his spare time: he learned a lot, and often called Constance his schoolmistress. He still worked in the House of Lords, but, having been non-political, he was becoming anti-political, against the governance of the old United Kingdom, more impressed by the American model of democratic capitalism, and ready and willing to devote time to international commerce. He was employed in the financial services industry and in a company that provided weather forecasts. He would listen with one ear to the urgings of his father-in-law Jim Burnett and his brother-in-law Hank to drop his titles, his English accent, come to Colorado and be a cowboy.

Two events forced him to think harder of the future, his own and his family's. Constance was pregnant with another baby, and, although she never said so, he realised that three children under six would call for a larger home and extra help, and that she would have loved to be more in Colorado if only he could have been there. The new baby was going to cause upheaval of one sort or another, far-reaching decisions lay ahead, and he would have to take into consideration the unsettled and unsettling atmosphere in his country. The second event was the law passed by the House of Commons to chuck the hereditary peers out of the House of Lords. The 'life' peers, lords only for the duration of their lives, would stay put, a number of hereditaries would be ousted immediately, the rest were to follow, and nobody knew what was to become of the so-called Upper House in the end.

The results of Theodore's cogitations and discussions with Constance were that he wrote a speech, his maiden speech; attended along with most of the other hereditaries the so-called 'farewell' debate; then, with a last glance up at Constance in the gallery, seized his chance and rose to his feet.

He began with the customary courtesies, and the burden of his speech was as follows.

'My lords, my maiden speech has been long in coming, but will be as short as possible.

'My lords, I apologise for the poor record of my family, generations of which seldom entered this House, some of which never voted, and only one of which, apart from myself, contributed to the donkey-work that is our chief responsibility.

'Yet I dare to claim that a nation benefits from persons entitled to influence the legislative process who are not professional politicians, are largely unpaid, and do not necessarily have the dangerous gift of the gab.

'My lords, I am one of the peers about to be expelled from this House because we inherited our titles. I am being penalised because I am the son of my father. I am subject to yet another of the laws which rule against the right of a father to give what is or was his to his son.

'My lords, I belong to no political party and am not a controversialist. But I do have a firm opinion on the matter, and am aware that any and every opinion can cause controversy. With regrets, I beg your indulgence for the opinions I feel compelled to air.

'The politicians who rule our country are empowered to confiscate a percentage, conceivably a hundred per cent, of the money we possess when we die, and the property. They have decided that our innate inclination to save our money and leave it to our children is not a right but a privilege. And now they tell me that I am not to keep the seat in the House of Lords and the right to sit in it conferred on my family by a former government hundreds of years ago, which was bequeathed to me by my father. If natural inclinations and ancient rights are privileges, and privileges are subject to the prejudice of politicians, why stop at our savings and our constitutional appointments? Politicians have not yet gone so far, but could rule that nothing worth anything is to pass from one generation to the next. Examples of possible further confiscations occur to me. Surely there could be objections to the surnames we have inherited: they are not titles, but they confer privilege – remember the poorest of poor little rich girls, who was spoilt by the whole world because she was the daughter of Stalin. And what about the faces we inherit? Beauty can be inherited and confers privileges without number – it should be defaced. Talent, again – talent, the greatest of all the privileges – the hands of writers, painters and musicians should be amputated, and the tongues of political prodigies cut out.

'The idea behind the abolition of hereditary peers in the House of Lords is that they are unelected and undemocratic. The civil servants on the taxpayers' pay-roll wield wide power, as do the arbiters of our fate on governmental committees and quangos: they are all unelected. Democracy is a fine word: but the 'people' do not have much say in the running of their homeland. They would not agree that their children should inherit nothing worth anything. They do not agree that evil murderers should be kept alive and in relative comfort and security for years or even for life at their expense.

'My lords, we belong to the twentieth century and, if you will forgive me for saying so, we are the children of Marxism, of Marxist theory, of communist practice, socialism and the left. Our country has been spared the excesses of tyrants and despots murdering tens of millions of their compatriots in the name of "the people" – spared so far, I would add. Yet our country has been brought low by the attempts of politicians to follow the instructions and realise the aims of Karl Marx, who did so much of his scribbling in the British Museum.

'I am no Marxist scholar, but then it is not scholarship that provokes revolution, it is a "cry", a rallying word or two. The cry of Marxism that has disgraced the twentieth century is: the class war. It has set man against man, sanctioned crime and excused sin. Our home-bred politicians of the left have acted, reacted and over-reacted in response to the declaration of the class war – and they have often been aped by liberals and politicians of the right. Doctrinaire and damaging theories and their application have been the consequence: for instance, that the creation of wealth matters less for a nation than the distribution of charity; again, that the elite, the best and most essential people in society, have to be reviled and degraded; again, that people are pleased to be taxed more heavily, for whatever reason; and again, that to level is to level up, when it always and only levels down.

'My lords, the twentieth century has by now proved that Marxism-communism-socialism makes the mistake of challenging human nature and misinterpreting nature itself in an omnipotent sense. It advertises the ideal of equality, promises heaven on earth or pie in the sky, and, having gained power, holds on to it by nothing but force. Egalitarianism does not figure in nature's world, and is not the bedrock of the human psyche. Along with the rest of creation, we are competitors for a living, we are hunters, we still are, and our hearts are not made to bleed exclusively for the welfare of the stupid, the sick, the idle, criminals and animals.

'Of course the purpose of civilisation is to ameliorate the law of the jungle; but it is unwise to reject the idea, and disregard the incontrovertible evidence, of the survival of the fittest. Conflict is literally the daily bread of nature – you eat your neighbour or you are eaten. In this House we have striven to check our instinct to do likewise; but I urge its new membership to remember that we forget the lessons of the wild at our peril. For nature not only warns against the sentimental and hypocritical manifesto of the left, it also demonstrates that war within a species, continuous war forming a way of life, is rare because it is intolerable, unbearable, as countries ruled on Marxist lines, by means of class war and ultimately by terror, have discovered to their cost.

'My lords, the government of the former Great Britain and the former United Kingdom, in pursuance of socialistic aims, has virtually ruined my family by taxation and is cancelling my ancestral right to expose its plots and plans in this House of Parliament. So be it! I may be insignificant, I consider myself insignificant, except as a straw in the wind of decadence. With regret I would add that for reasons personal as well as political I shall disclaim my titles, of Gorham and Gorhambury, and renounce my citizenship of my changed and diminished native land.'

The Gorhamburys and their three children, the two boys and Millicent known as Milly, had emigrated to the USA. They were now settled in the house built to their own specifications in the small town of Wagonway, a few miles from the Burnett farm and the Burnett family and the new Burnett business. Not long after Theodore's one and only speech in the House of Lords, a vein of gold was discovered on land owned by Constance's father. It was nothing like the gold-strike at Cripple Creek in the 1890s, but rich enough to be exploited commercially. Jim Burnett and Hank needed someone with experience of high finance to help them set up Wagonway Gold Inc., and had invited Theodore to fill the post. Both Theodore and Constance worked respectively full-time and part-time for the company, and their earnings sufficed for all their needs. In many ways, and on the whole, they were happier than they had been in England.

One morning a letter with printing on the envelope arrived at Woody, the name of their home. Theodore thought it was junk mail, but Constance managed to stop him throwing it away unopened. It was from the editor of a magazine called *Yesterday Today*, a high-class historical quarterly with offices in New York. The letter was addressed to the Marquess of Gorhambury and signed Richard E. Harley. Mr Harley requested an interview and offered an irresistibly large sum of money for an hour or two of Theodore's time. He already seemed to know a lot about Widells past and present, gave an outline of his proposed questioning, and promised that Lord Gorhambury would be able to cut any part of the text in proof that he preferred not to publicise.

Theodore agreed – he was not above accepting money for jam. At 10 a.m. on a Saturday he greeted Mr Harley and a young man, Bert, bearing electrical equipment. Mr Harley, who wished to be called Richard, was middle-aged, balding, in rimless glasses, keen, polite and typical of the American erudite class. Bert was overweight and speechless. The interview was recorded by Bert in Theodore's study, which would be quiet after the telephone was disconnected.

It began by Richard asking: 'Sir, am I right to address you as Lord Gorhambury?'

'You're right and wrong. You would have been right in days gone by, when I lived in England, but you're wrong since I now live here in Colorado.'

'How should I address you, sir?'

'I use only my family name. You know that I disclaimed my titles some years ago? However, my wife and my friends have given me a Yankee nickname, which, as could be said, covers a multitude of sins. They write it M-a-r-q-u-i-s and pronounce it in French with an American twang – Markee, like that. I suggest that in our conversation you call me Markee, and leave it to you to choose how to present me in the printed form.'

'Thank you sir. May I begin by welcoming you to my country, and saying how proud we are that you wish to become an American citizen.'

'Thank you, Richard.'

'Could I ask if your children are going to be Americans?'

'My sons are being educated at my old schools, and we feel they must decide for themselves whether they want to be Americans or to remain Englishmen. My daughter has begun her education in Colorado and will probably stick to American schooling.'

'Your family, Markee – your recorded family history dates back to the time of Queen Elizabeth the First, I believe?'

'So they say.'

'When does your family first figure in extant documents?'

'I don't know, I've never taken much interest in history, which is mostly fiction in my view. The family papers are stored in the Records Office at Gorham.'

'There is a story, Markee, that your "original" forefather was connected with a tree?'

'Correct.'

'A tree in the Forest of Woody?'

'The Forest belonged to us for a long time.'

'Is that why you have called your home Woody?'

'Probably.'

'Do you think the nursery of your family was woodland?'

'That's apocryphal – not proven.'

'But it's fact, not fiction, that the surname of the founding father was Widdle?'

'True.'

'Meaning urine in the vernacular?'

'I'd be grateful if you didn't make too much of it, Richard.'

'Point taken, Markee. But, for the record, may I continue to seek answers to my prepared list of questions?'

'You can try.'

'Widdle was the name or the word applied to the man whose widow found your forebear?'

'According to the story.'

'When and why did the spelling change?'

'Richard, you are to be congratulated on the purity of your mind. Widdle is not a nice name to have to carry through a world of smut.'

'I beg pardon, Markee. I was asking for academic reasons.'

'Oh well – why is obvious – when is established in some old document. Heiresses are often the making of families like mine, they hoist their husbands up the ladder of advancement, and money's the father and mother of snobbery, and no snob would be happy to call himself or be called Widdle.'

'Do you refer to your namesake, Markee, Theodore the First, who married the Dunbee heiress?'

'I was generalising.'

'But Ann Dunbee was loaded, as we say in the States, and the first Theodore's name was already changed to Widell when he married her. No doubt, for dignity's sake, the pronunciation was altered at the same time.'

'You know more about these things than I do, Richard.'

'Thank you, sir. But I'm sure you know that your namesake hit the jackpot, if I may put it so crudely, in the form of Miss Dunbee?'

'I do. And I'd like to take this opportunity to register gratitude to the lady on behalf of my forebears, although some of them did their damnedest by means of folly or in one case deliberately to rid themselves of their wealth.'

'The vicissitudes of your family wealth are as intriguing as its fortunes in the sense of the acquisition of power and influence. But for the moment, with your approval, Markee, I would prefer to follow the latter route. Your family achieved noble status. According to certain historical texts, it was again the doing of a lady – no pun intended. Would you agree?'

'Are you thinking of another brief encounter?'

'A brief encounter with a difference: it was with King Charles the Second?'

'He spent one night in what was then our home.'

'And paid for his pleasure?'

'Regally he rewarded his host, which benefited his hostess.'

'She bore a child?'

'His name can be found on our family tree.'

'Of course, sir. He created your ancestor Baron Gorham, and gave your ancestress, and subsequent Ladies of Gorham, the right to inherit the title. I imagine the lady in question was pretty and loyal?'

'Reputedly.'

'But the child she bore did not survive?'

'No.'

'She had another?'

'Oh yes, a Widell from top to toe, more brawn than brain, I gather.'

'But he carried on the line. He was to lead to your Victorian forebear, who was raised to a higher rank in the nobility of England, and eventually to your good self. What is so interesting to Americans, Markee, and indeed to the readers of *Yesterday Today*, is the rise of the aristocratic families of the UK and Europe throughout the centuries. We love to hear and read about families that have not only transformed themselves, encouraging the rest of us to hope to do likewise, but have also retained their wealth and maintained their pomp and their prestige up to the here-and-now.'

'Richard, look again – pomp and prestige have gone the way of Gorhambury and the Forest of Woody – from Widell back to Widdle, to your compatriot, Hiram Widdle. But I don't want to disillusion you. Whatever name aristocracy hides under nowadays, the value of breeding, of trying to produce a better man just as farmers and the horse-racing fraternity try to produce a better animal, is common sense and unarguable. I believe in that principle along with other unfashionable things – but we'd both have to admit that the first "aristocrat" to bear the name of Widdle was a baby found in a bag tied to the branch of a tree – and after that our aristocratic pretensions were maintained fortuitously.'

At this point an aeroplane flew low over the house and noise spoilt the recording. Then Bert's equipment developed a fault, and Richard had to scribble on a clipboard as his questions were answered.

Theodore illustrated his theme by reference to his translation from an English ex-grandee, ex-peer of that realm, and ex-job-seeker, into the executive of an American mining company by virtue of his encountering an American girl who had strayed into London. His marriage to Constance and the discovery of gold on agricultural land were unfathomable coincidences. The waywardness of fortune, or for that matter life, was exemplified again by the death in infancy of his twin and elder brother Oscar, briefly Marquess of Gorhambury, and his own inheritance of the titles and so on.

He then explained that he had never known his mother, that his father was not exactly virile, and the birth of Oscar and himself was a mystery, if not so fraught with problems as the rivalry of the other Widell twins in the distant past. He said the family VC was won more by foul temper than by heroism. He suggested the Marquessate was ultimately a reward for having charmed Queen Victoria; and that the South Sea Bubble money was the ill-gotten gain of an addiction to gambling.

Constance now supplied the three men with refreshments. She laughed to hear that Theodore had been denigrating his ancestors, and volunteered contradictory information and opinions. By the time she left the study, Bert was again ready to record and the interview was drawing to a close.

Richard asked: 'Would you care to comment on the state of the American nation, Markee?'

'I would not, I wouldn't presume – my application for citizenship expresses my sentiments in respect of your country.'

'How would you compare America with yours?'

'The latter's in a bad way at present, but at least for the time being it's a monarchy, despite the efforts of envy and spite to destroy the royal family, for instance by legislating against the old rules of inheritance – a king or a queen elected for life is a contradiction in terms. Royalty differs from aristocracy. Although kings and queens may win their crowns by force of arms or the accumulation of gold, once they have been crowned and anointed before God they acquire a mystical significance. Bolshies don't recognise mystic or spiritual values. They cut off the heads of kings or shoot tsars in cellars, and bring about the unintended consequences of the restoration of King Charles the Second, the coronation of Napoleon, and the reigns of that impostor Lenin and the other homicidal maniac, Stalin. People love a loveable royal leader, so perhaps England won't sink into the sea. But comparisons are odious, and in answer to your question I would just say that constitutional monarchies dilute the power of politicians, are usually pleasant to live in, and are a better bargain for taxpayers than presidential elections and upheaval every few years.'

'Does this bring us to your speech in the House of Lords, Markee?'

'Water under the bridge, Richard.'

'You were critical of the country of your birth.'

'I was saddened by it.'

'Do you believe decadence is unstoppable?'

'How long does it take to thin out a population, how can you cease to provide welfare, how do you persuade the masses not to be improvident, how do you restore the profit motive, instil the principle of self-help, resurrect religion?'

'I would beg to disagree, sir. You have urged me to look at yourself, and I have done so, and see that you are reinventing your family on alien soil with resourcefulness and energy. You are doing what you say a modern nation cannot do. I hope that your resurgence suggests a possible cure for ills that affect many of us and quite a few countries.'

'Hope's free, Richard – and we're living in a free capitalist country.'

'Not completely free, Markee – alas, we are slaves of the clock. I must forgo the pleasure of your company, but not before expressing an opinion of my own. You spoke of breeding, and I feel that you are living proof of the advantages of that theory. For my sins, Markee, I am a devotee of the turf. Please take what I am about to say in the complimentary spirit intended: you have convinced me that you will have bred winners and that your issue will shed further lustre on your family.'

Theodore laughed and replied: 'Thank you, Richard – it's nice to know that you value me as a sire if less so as a sir. I, too, have an opinion to express. Please remember that it's a wise son who knows his father. My mother was called Goodbody on my Birth Certificate – I understand she chose that name because it suited her – and my guess is that many men could have vouched for her generosity. I hope I am not what I am, or used to be, by false pretences. Anyway, I'm proud to claim to be like my putative forefathers in at least one particular – survivability. My speech in the House of Lords embarrasses me nowadays, because I spoke of the ruin of my family. It was accurate enough at the time, but no longer. You will remember that Jesus said: "The poor always ye have with you," a depressing sentence for levellers, but not so depressing as its corollary: the rich always ye have with you. Several predecessors of mine strove to get rid of their wealth, and failed. They wished in vain for the one thing they had not got, poverty. But I have been poor enough to appreciate money. Thank you for studying my family – it's flattering – but I'm inclined to think we're really not worth writing home about. Only a couple of the patriarchs were meritorious, the foundling and the marquess – and there would have been no marquess if the foundling had perished as intended in that bag. Nevertheless, despite exceptions that prove the rule, we have all been more or less wealthy and endowed with the power of wealth. The point is, the interesting aspect of us is, why? Why have we survived at or near the top of the tree when other families fall by the wayside and have no history to speak of? Who knows? Who knows anything important? My own answer, for what it's worth, is – chance. You yourself, Richard, like it or not, will be playing the game of chance if or when you refer to me in *Yesterday Today*: is the blood in my veins authentic Widdle? As for my family, we won some games of chance – that's the beginning and end of our story.'